Dining with Danger

"Did you enjoy your walk in the woods?" Naomi asked.

"You could say that . . . ," George started. Nancy kicked her beneath the table.

"Actually, it's beautiful here at that time of day," Nancy said.

"You guys might like to try one of my wild-food harvest tours while you're here. I'm actually the in-residence herbalist, wild-food specialist, and assistant gardener during the growing season. I just wait tables for the winter," she said.

"We just might do that!" Nancy said.

A few minutes later Naomi returned to the table with fresh rolls and drinks for the girls and Hannah. But all at once the lights went out. Startled, Naomi bumped the table and a wineglass flew out of her hand. The sound of glass shattering was followed by a shrill shriek.

Nancy Drew
Mystery Stories

Available from Simon & Schuster

NANCY DREW® 174

A TASTE OF DANGER

CAROLYN KEENE

Aladdin Paperbacks
New York   London   Toronto   Sydney   Singapore

This book is a work of fiction. Any references to historical events, real people, or real locales are used fictitiously. Other names, characters, places, and incidents are the product of the author's imagination, and any resemblance to actual events or locales or persons, living or dead, is entirely coincidental.

First Aladdin Paperbacks edition September 2003

Copyright © 2003 by Simon & Schuster, Inc.

ALADDIN PAPERBACKS
An imprint of Simon & Schuster
Children's Publishing Division
1230 Avenue of the Americas
New York, NY 10020

Printed in the United States of America

10 9 8 7 6 5 4 3 2 1

NANCY DREW, NANCY DREW MYSTERY STORIES, and colophon are registered trademarks of Simon & Schuster, Inc.

Library of Congress Control Number 2003101088

ISBN 0-689-86154-0

Contents

1

A Close Shave

"Oh, Nancy," Bess Marvin said from the backseat of the rented minivan. She held a colorful brochure in her hands, and her eyes glowed with excitement. "You won't believe who the guest chef of the month is at the Gourmet Getaway!"

Nancy Drew glanced briefly away from the winding blacktop to the reflection of her friend in the rearview mirror. "At the moment I'm not sure I care—unless he or she sends a search party to find us!" Irritated, Nancy blew a strand of her thick red-blond hair off her face. She was not the kind of person who got lost easily. But somehow she'd taken a wrong turn off the interstate and was now hopelessly lost in the middle of the Berkshire Mountains. To make things worse, she found that the whole area was a dead zone for her cell phone when she tried to call the Getaway for better directions. She hoped she could find her way out of the maze of back roads before dark.

"I've seen him on that cable cooking network!" Hannah Gruen, the Drews' housekeeper, spoke up from her seat next to Bess. Hannah, Bess, Nancy, and Bess's cousin, George Fayne, had been invited to spend a week at the trendy new resort in western Massachusetts. "He's one of the world's great chefs— though I do take issue with the last biscuit recipe he had on his show."

"Biscuits, smishkits!" George groaned, looking up from the road atlas. George was sitting in the front passenger seat, trying to navigate Nancy through a set of very confusing directions to the resort. "If we don't get where we're going soon, I'm going to scream. Nancy, what is the name of that town at the bottom of the hill? Maybe it's on the map."

"Waringham. We passed the sign about a tenth of a mile back. Population's only eight hundred and three," Nancy said.

Nancy slowed the blue van to a crawl and anxiously peered at the few stores lining the road. To her left was a post office, to her right a little 1950s-style gas station with a single pump and a sign reading CLOSED: GONE HUNTING!

Beyond the station was a larger store. "'Waringham

2

General Store: Victuals, Dry Goods, Camping Gear,'"
Bess read aloud. "What are victuals, anyway?"

"Food!" George replied, peering through the window. "They're open, Nan. Let's stop and ask directions."

"Before we get even more lost," Nancy agreed.

"This place looks like a ghost town," Bess observed as Nancy parked the van.

"A very *well kept* ghost town!" Hannah chuckled. "I bet beneath its humble surface this village is pretty upscale. That antique store looks pricey. And this general store has some expensive gourmet foods in the window. I remember when general stores sold canned meats and sturdy jeans!"

"As long as someone in there can give me directions, I don't care if they're ghosts *or* gourmets." Nancy took the map and sheet of e-mailed directions from George. "I'll be back in a sec," she promised, unsnapping her seat belt.

Nancy zipped up her blue fleece hooded jacket and jogged up the wooden steps of the old-fashioned store. She pushed open the door and looked around. The store was larger than it seemed from the outside. A U-shaped counter divided the store—on one side there were food items and on the other side were all sorts of clothing and gear. A locked glass case displayed hunting rifles, knives, and bows and arrows. Apparently the locals took hunting season seriously!

3

The shopkeeper smiled. "Can I help you?"

"I hope so." Nancy handed him the directions to Gourmet Getaway. "We're lost. I know we're somewhere near Rabbit Run Road, but I can't find it on our map."

"Because it's only on local maps!" the shopkeeper said. He quickly sketched a little map on the back of Nancy's directions. "It's about five miles away. Just make a left at the crossroads and go straight for four miles. Hang a right, and you'll soon see the entrance gate on your left. Can't miss it. Nice place, and good customers," he added.

Nancy thanked the man and headed back to the van. About fifteen minutes later the friends spotted the first sign for the resort. Another quarter mile and they were at the gate.

Nancy made a left onto the winding gravel drive. Soon they were in front of a large, old-fashioned Victorian-era hotel. A generous porch ran around the sprawling, white three-story building. Green shutters framed the windows; bunches of colorful Indian corn hung from the porch railing.

Nancy parked near the main entrance. Moments after she climbed out, a bald-headed man carrying a stack of firewood walked toward them. "Mike Rinaldi here." He introduced himself while casting an anxious look at the van.

Nancy looked quickly from the man back to the

4

van to see if something was wrong. "Uh—Mr. Rinaldi, I'm Nancy Drew and—"

Mike didn't let her finish. He put the firewood down, grabbed her wrist, and pumped her hand vigorously. "Carson Drew's daughter! I should have recognized you. Though I haven't seen you since you were maybe five or six years old. You've grown into quite the young woman," he said, his face brightening with a warm grin that made Nancy like him instantly.

Then he noticed Hannah. "Hannah Gruen! You haven't changed a bit," he said, warmly sandwiching her hands between his.

"It's been ages," Hannah replied. "I still remember when you came to the house for dinner once—back when Nancy was a little girl. Mr. Drew sends his regards and wishes he could have made the trip—though frankly, I'm delighted he sent me in his stead." She scanned the beautifully landscaped grounds. Most of the trees were already bare, but a few bronze leaves rattled from the oaks fringing the drive.

While introducing Bess and George to him, Nancy realized she *did* vaguely remember Mike. He looked the same, except he hadn't been totally bald back then. She also could picture his wife, Lauren— now his ex-wife. She was a sparkly, dark-haired woman who had spent most of the long-ago visit trading recipes with Hannah. Nancy's dad had told her that Mike and Lauren had divorced a couple of years ago, and he was now remarried to someone named Jillian.

They quickly unpacked the van. Mike grabbed a couple of their bags and called a worker to help bring their things into the hotel. "Put these in the two adjoining rooms on the second floor in the west wing," he instructed his employee, then turned back to Nancy. "Jillian and I opened the Gourmet Getaway last June," he told them as they entered the building. The lobby opened on one side onto a spacious dining room, where a young woman was already setting the tables for dinner. A delicate but enticing aroma filled the air. Nancy's stomach rumbled with hunger. Lunch had been a bag of popcorn and some soda.

On the other side of the lobby, to the left of a winding staircase, an arched entryway led to the hotel lounge. Guests were nestled in overstuffed chairs and sofas, reading or talking. Nancy fell in love with the comfortable mixture of dark Victorian and elegant New England colonial style furniture.

"You've sure got a good crowd for this time of year," Hannah remarked.

Mike nodded as he returned from the registration desk. "It usually wouldn't be—but we've come up with a way to draw people between the busy seasons. We have this gimmick: guest chef of the month."

"Louis Cadot!" Bess chirped. "He's fantastic. No wonder you've got this crowd."

"Plus, we managed to snare him during the height of hunting season. Now we're all booked up for the next couple of weeks!"

Just then there was a commotion at the front door. Mike looked past Nancy and frowned. "Now who is this?" he wondered aloud.

Nancy followed his gaze. Two women and a mustached man had walked in the door. They were carrying their own bags, and looked a bit put out.

"It's the Sanchez party," a quiet voice spoke up. Nancy turned to face a willowy blond woman. She was thirty-something, model slim, and had a familiar face.

Bess's eyes grew wide. "You're Jillian Coatley. . . . You've been on the cover of *High Style!*" she gasped.

Nancy couldn't help but stare. Of course she'd heard the name before. Who hadn't? And now she could place that face. Jillian Coatley was one of fashion's supermodels. She'd retired from modeling a couple of years ago.

"Now Jillian *Rinaldi,*" the blonde said with a shy smile. "Mike and I are married. But yes, I used to be 'Coatley.'" She touched Mike's arm. "The Sanchezes booked at the last minute and drove up from New York. We've put them in the west wing near the Drew party's rooms."

7

"That's us!" Bess said, looking as if she were about to ask Jillian for her autograph. Nancy cleared her throat and caught Bess's eye. Bess grinned.

"Oh, so you're Carson's family and friends! Welcome. I'm sorry he couldn't make it. I was looking forward to meeting him. You must be Hannah Gruen," she said, turning to Hannah. "And from what I've heard of your cooking, you're in for a really good time here."

Everyone was quickly introduced, then Jillian turned to Mike. "The Sanchezes seemed a little demanding on the phone, plus they're about three hours late—they told us they'd be here for lunch. Why don't you attend to them personally—smooth some feathers? I can show Nancy and her friends to their rooms and then give them the grand tour."

Mike agreed, handed Jillian the keys to the rooms, and hurried off to speak with the newly arrived guests. Just as he extended his hand to greet them, he tripped over one of their bags. Jillian gasped as Mr. Sanchez grabbed Mike's arm to stop him from falling head-on into one of the lobby's potted plants.

"Poor Mike," Jillian murmured, leading the way to the stairs. "He's a wreck."

Nancy glanced back at the resort owner. He was guiding the Sanchezes to the registration desk. Though she couldn't overhear what he was saying, she could tell from his body language that he was talking

8

too fast, obviously embarrassed by his awkward greeting. "He does seem a bit nervous," she agreed.

"We all are! There's a rumor that a food critic from the *Offbeat and Great Eats Travel Guide* is visiting here this week."

"Oh, that's such a great travel book," Bess remarked. "Who's the critic?"

Jillian made a face. "Who knows? He or she is a mystery. Their critic, like several others who write for top publications, has a pseudonym. So there's no way of knowing who it is. And to top it off, I'm worried because they're coming at Lauren Rinaldi's invitation."

"Mike's ex-wife?" Nancy blurted out, then bit her lip.

Jillian patted her arm. "It's okay. It's a pretty amicable divorce—or it was until we opened this place. Anyway, Lauren has connections in the gourmet food community. She's *supposedly* doing us a favor by having a critic come," Jillian concluded. She showed them to their doors and arranged to meet them in fifteen minutes down in the lobby for a tour of the rest of the inn. She handed over keys to Nancy and Hannah, who were sharing the larger of two adjacent rooms, and to Bess and George, who were next door. Then she politely excused herself.

"That's pretty weird," Bess remarked as they watched Jillian retreat down the hall. "Having your ex-wife send a critic to review your new business venture."

"You'd think Lauren would at least clue Mike in as to who was coming. You know, give him a bit of a break," George said.

"Maybe Lauren really is doing them a favor, and the critic will give the inn good press," Nancy mused aloud.

"Why do the critics bother with all the secrecy?" George asked as Nancy opened the door to her room.

"Because when they review a restaurant, they want to see what the everyday food and service are like," Hannah explained. "They don't want the chef and staff to make a special effort. That wouldn't give an accurate picture of how good the restaurant really is."

"So they travel incognito!" Nancy said, finding the thought very appealing. It would be fun trying to figure out who the food critic was.

They went into their rooms to freshen up. Nancy and George changed into sweats and sneakers, hoping to have time for a walk at the end of Jillian's tour of the grounds. A few minutes later they headed for the stairs, and ran into the Sanchezes in the hall.

"You heading off for the grand tour?" the mustached man asked. He was of medium height, with black hair and a friendly smile. "Oh, I'm Oscar Sanchez. This is my wife, Isabelle," he said, taking the arm of an attractive woman with honey-blond hair. "And this is my sister, Monica." Monica's mane of hair was as dark as her brother's, but she had a very fair complexion. She was, Nancy decided, any-one's definition of beautiful—or would be, if she didn't look so generally annoyed!

"Yes, though I hope it doesn't take too long," Nancy answered. "We drove from River Heights to Chicago, flew to Boston, and have been driving all day. We need a major hike before dinner."

"Getting lost made the trip even longer," George pointed out.

Monica's scowl deepened. "See, Oscar, what did I tell you? It was the directions. They were amateur-ish, and downright dumb."

"You have to forgive Monica," Isabelle spoke up quickly. "She was hoping to have a decent lunch, and instead we ate peanut butter crackers from a vending machine."

"And we're three hours later than we planned," Monica added. "Let's get this tour over with. I want to take a good hot bath before dinner."

Jillian met up with all of them back in the lobby. "Since it's late and I know some of you want to rest up or take a walk, I'll just give you the high points of the grand tour," she began, leading them down the back hall and toward the source of the wonderful aroma that Nancy had noticed earlier. "As you know," she continued, "part of the fun of Gourmet Getaway is that guests are free to take cooking classes given by the chef and learn some tricks of the trade."

"And free not to, I hope," Monica said, rolling her eyes.

"Ms. Sanchez, you are free to spend the day any way you want. We have spa facilities for your comfort, as well as lots of outdoor activities. The trails are open for hikers, and we have miles of scenic paths if you want to explore the countryside on horseback," Jillian added with a trace of tightness in her voice.

Nancy admired her patience. Monica was obviously being a pill about their late arrival. What in the world was she doing here anyway?

Oscar quickly answered her unvoiced question. "Jillian, don't mind my sister. She just needs a good meal and a good night's sleep, and her mood will improve."

"Sorry. Didn't mean to sound like such a grump," Monica apologized.

"Well, here's a sight that should cheer you up," Jillian said, opening the hall door and stepping aside for the party to enter the kitchen.

The place smelled wonderful and positively sparkled. The stainless steel surfaces of counters, cooktops, ovens, and refrigerators gleamed, and the pots and pans suspended from ceiling racks were mirror bright. Everything was so spotless that even Hannah, ever the critic of restaurant cleanliness, was impressed.

Chef Cadot wasn't around, but several helpers in

immaculate white chef's hats and uniforms were busy chopping vegetables, sauteeing onions, and stirring the contents of several pots. The atmosphere was calm, but very busy and focused. The workers barely looked up as the party passed through into the well-stocked pantry near the back door.

A narrow hallway led past the restaurant office, where meals were planned and provisions were ordered. Jillian pointed out that besides two walk-in refrigerators there was an old icehouse outside, and a root cellar that was accessible now only from the outside. Before the inn was renovated there was a passage directly from the pantry to the root cellar. It had been sealed ages ago, in the early 1900s. From the back door she pointed out the gardens, now rusty with frost; a modest greenhouse that supplied the fresh herbs and greens through the winter; and the chef's cottage.

At the end of the tour Bess and Hannah opted to hang out in the kitchen with Isabelle and Oscar and watch the chef prepare dinner. Yawning and bored, Monica headed back to her room. Nancy and George stuck to their original plan and went for their walk.

The wind was up, but a pale November sun had broken through the clouds low over the western horizon, and the sky was clearing. Nancy tucked her hands into her pockets. "Which way?" she asked George.

George glanced at the Getaway brochure she'd

tucked in her jacket and pointed to the left of a corral and the stables. "Over there. We'd better get a move on. I'd say there's only about twenty minutes of daylight left. That's ten into the woods, and ten back again."

"More than enough time if we walk quickly," Nancy said, hurrying to keep up with George. As Nancy passed the greenhouse, she slowed her pace a bit and shielded her eyes to see inside.

"Watch out!" a voice cried.

Nancy looked up quickly. She saw a tall, slim girl on the path, carrying a heavy bushel basket brimming with fist-sized pumpkins. On top of the orange vegetables were several bunches of fresh herbs. Except for her long dark hair she was plain-looking, with hazel eyes and a washed-out complexion. Beneath a shabby red down vest, she was wearing a cook's white cotton jacket and pants. She looked cold and tired. Nancy stepped aside to let her pass, and smiled. "Need a hand?"

The girl didn't return her smile. "No, I can manage." She hastened toward the kitchen door, then, as an afterthought, turned. "But thanks." Still no smile.

George had jogged back to Nancy. "Who's that?"

Nancy shrugged. "She seems to have been gathering part of dinner from the garden. She didn't seem too friendly." She looked over her shoulder as they resumed their walk. The girl was at the kitchen door,

14

talking to a guy Nancy had noticed earlier prepping vegetables.

A few minutes later Nancy and George crossed a meadow and found the trail leading into the woods. Even with the trees all bare, the light in the forest was dim. "I don't know how far we should go," George said, checking her watch.

Nancy put her hand in her pocket and pulled out a flashlight. "Don't worry. Even if the sun sets before we get back, I have this. And Mike told us the grounds are well lit at night." Nancy slowed her pace and drew a deep breath. "It smells wonderful here, and I love the feel of this place. Let's keep going for a while, and . . ."

George put her finger on Nancy's lips, silencing her. She pointed into a glade to the right. Shafts of sun slanted low over the surface of a shallow woodland pond. Standing at the edge of the pond, silhouetted by the light, was a deer. Its graceful neck was bent low over the water, its head hidden by a thicket. When it lifted its head, Nancy saw it had an impressive rack of antlers. It was a buck. His nose twitched, and he stomped his right forefoot.

"Something's spooked it," Nancy whispered.

The words were barely out of her mouth when a figure rose from the brush on the other side of the pond, upwind of the deer. It was a man wielding a bow and arrow. He took aim, and suddenly an arrow came whizzing right toward George's head.

2

Recipe for Disaster

"George, watch out!" Nancy yelled, then tackled her friend. As the arrow whizzed over their heads they landed in the brambles. The arrow was instantly followed by an infuriated cry.

"What was that?" George gasped as Nancy tried to catch her breath.

She didn't bother to answer. She jumped up, pulling at the leaves snared in her hair. "You almost killed us!" Nancy yelled at the figure barreling down the path toward her.

"*You* had no right to be here," the man shouted back. He was carrying his bow in one hand and had a quiver filled with arrows attached to his belt. The man was burly and was about the meanest-looking person Nancy had encountered in a long time.

Certainly the smelliest. He was unshaven, dirty, and definitely not the sort of person two girls wanted to meet alone in the woods at twilight.

Nancy was too angry to care. "We have every right to be here," she countered. "We're guests at the Getaway. This is the Rinaldis' land. *You're* the one who is trespassing."

"And you certainly had no right to shoot at us," George spoke up. She was holding the man's arrow. Its point was a double-edged blade. She made no move to return it.

"Shooting at you?" the man scoffed. "More like at the twelve-point buck you spooked."

"You aim right at us and you're worried about losing a chance at a deer?" Nancy fumed. "This is unbelievable! I'm reporting you to the police for trespassing. Come on, George." Nancy grabbed George's elbow and started briskly back down the path.

"Trespassing?" the man repeated scornfully, and stomped right up to them. Stepping in front of Nancy, he barred their way. He glared at the girls. "*You're* who's trespassing. Those idiots at that lodge— like all the rest of those know-it-alls who come here from New York or Boston—are the ones who don't belong here. And let me tell you, no one has more right to this land and the game here than me, Nate Caldwell. Now give me my arrow back and scram!"

17

With that, he yanked the arrow from George's hand, and stalked noisily into the bushes. After a moment there was silence.

"Walk; don't run!" Nancy whispered. She and George marched defiantly out of the woods. Only when they were clear of the forest did they start to run for the lodge.

Once inside, George sank back against the wall. "That was beyond scary, Nan!"

"He was way out of line," Nancy agreed. Her heart was still pounding. She'd had a good scare, but now she was more angry than afraid. "Mike's going to hear about this Nate guy."

"Let's change and call the police," George said, starting up the back stairs to the second floor.

When she was upstairs, Nancy stopped outside her door. She was beginning to calm down. "George, on second thought, we'd better speak to Mike first. It'll look bad to have the police descend on this place during dinner. I don't think Nate Caldwell is going very far. He seems to think he has a right to live right there in the woods—or at least nearby."

By the time they had changed for dinner, Nancy had decided to put off talking to Mike until even later, when he was finished working for the evening. He had enough to worry about with the prospect of a critic lurking about the premises.

• • •

"So what do you think of the hors d'oeuvres?" Bess asked, an anxious note in her voice.

The three girls and Hannah were seated comfortably at a corner table in the spacious dining room. As at most resorts, guests were assigned fixed tables for the duration of their stay. Mike had obviously given them one of the best tables. They had a view of the Berkshire Mountains that included, on a clear day, the region's highest peak, Mount Greylock.

"Why do I feel this is some kind of trick question?" George teased, then sampled some pâté. "Wow, I never thought I'd like chopped liver this much!" she commented, and heaped some more on a piece of toast.

"Monsieur Cadot himself complimented Bess on those carrot curls. Which I do admit look very professional, Bess." Hannah tore a piece off a warm French roll and spread it with some seasoned butter. "Bess and I actually ended up as part of the cooking class that met right after our kitchen tour," Hannah explained.

"That sounds like fun," Nancy commented, half wishing she'd stayed in the kitchen too and avoided meeting Nate. But at the moment, she intended to put all that unpleasantness out of mind—at least until after she enjoyed what promised to be a good dinner. "Monsieur Cadot's cooking lesson certainly seems to have suited Bess," she observed, looking at her friend. Bess's cheeks were pinker than usual, her eyes were glowing, and she'd fussed with her hair and makeup for an hour before donning her best pink mohair sweater. It didn't take Nancy's talent for solving mysteries to figure out that Bess's good mood had little to do with cooking lessons.

"Oh, the class was wonderful," Bess exclaimed.

"It was, and I'm surprised you did such a good job, considering the whole time you kept one eye on the chef's helper," Hannah added wryly.

"*One* eye!" Bess scoffed good-naturedly. "More like two eyes! That Ryan Logan is too hot to handle."

"Which one was he?" George asked.

"The five-foot-ten hunk, with blond hair and lashes to die for." Bess sighed.

"Is everything okay?" Mike Rinaldi asked as he stepped up to their table.

"Oh, it's great," Nancy assured him.

"Cadot outdid himself tonight," Mike told them, sounding pleased. "All three dinner seatings are booked. We're packed. I love it! Though it *is* a bit nerveracking," he added, lowering his voice. "I heard that Jillian told you about the food critic. What if he or she is here? It's so hard to keep everything running smoothly when we're so busy." Just then several guests entered the dining room, and Mike started over to greet them. Before he left, though, he said, "Let's talk later in the lounge over coffee. I want to catch up on all of Carson's news."

"If the entrées are as good as these appetizers," Nancy said when he was gone, "I don't think he has much to worry about." She looked around. "I also wonder if the critic is here yet."

"It would be fun guessing who it is," George said.

"I think it's that nice man Mr. Sanchez," Bess ventured in a low voice.

The Sanchezes were sitting nearby, at one of the other prime window seats. Obviously, Nancy realized, Mr. Rinaldi was going out of his way to smooth their feathers, just as Jillian had requested. The waiter had just brought their appetizers, and each member of their party had something different. Mr. Sanchez barely waited for the server to leave before sampling his shrimp. He offered one to his sister. She took a delicate bite and nodded. Nancy couldn't hear her, but she seemed to be pleased. Maybe the good food here would improve her mood.

"Why in the world do you think Mr. Sanchez is the critic?" Hannah wondered.

"The mustache. It looks fake!"

Nancy almost choked with laughter. "Really, Bess— isn't that a bit obvious for a disguise?"

"Maybe not," George mused. "Maybe he thinks we would think that and dismiss it."

"Not that he knows we're playing 'guess the food critic' here!" Nancy pointed out.

Just then their waiter walked up, an order pad in

her hand. "Hello, I'm Naomi, your server for the evening." It was the girl Nancy had seen earlier coming out of the garden. With her hair pinned up, and in pressed black trousers and a white ruffled shirt, Naomi definitely looked pretty. Especially when she smiled. She noticed Nancy and shyly acknowledged her. "Did you enjoy your walk in the woods?" she asked.

"You could say that . . . ," George started. Nancy kicked her beneath the table.

"Actually, it's beautiful here at that time of day," Nancy said.

"You guys might like to try one of my wild-food harvest tours while you're here. I'm actually the in-residence herbalist, wild-food specialist, and assistant gardener during the growing season. I just wait tables for the winter," she said.

"We just might do that!" Nancy said.

Naomi told them the specials of the evening. As she went back to the kitchen, George patted Bess's arm. "Hate to say this, but I think our waitress has a thing for Ryan."

"She does!" Bess stated this calmly, which surprised Nancy. "But they aren't an item. I know all about Ryan and Naomi. I talked to one of the other assistants about the two of them. Apparently Ryan's a bit of a rebel with a cause. He's charming, but more interested in saving the animals than dating right now. He's a real persuasive guy who supposedly has Naomi under his spell. I know the feeling!" Bess sighed.

A few minutes later Naomi returned to the table with fresh rolls and drinks for the girls and Hannah. But all at once the lights went out. Startled, Naomi bumped the table, and a wineglass flew out of her hand. The sound of glass shattering was followed by a shrill shriek.

3

An Unwelcome Guest

"My sweater! It's ruined." Bess's wail rose over the chorus of startled cries rising from various corners of the dining room.

"Be careful of that glass," Nancy warned, feeling for her purse. Groping inside, she found her penlight. She flicked it on, aiming the narrow beam first at Bess and then at the floor beside the table. Shards of glass glittered on the floor. "Just don't step back," Nancy cautioned as Bess stood up and began dabbing at her sweater.

"It's ruined," Bess said glumly. Her words were immediately echoed by a heavily accented voice that came from the direction of the kitchen.

"Ruined, everything is ruined!" The exclamation was followed by a string of angry French sentences.

24

"Poor Monsieur Cadot," said one guest.

"More like, poor us!" Even in the dark Nancy recognized Monica's voice. "First there was that poor excuse for lunch on the road. Now this. Great start to our gourmet weekend. We might as well head out for the nearest fast-food joint!"

"What a pain," George said under her breath. Nancy was about to agree when Naomi appeared, holding a lit candle in one hand and a glass of seltzer water in the other. She set the tall taper in the center of the table. "This should help," she said, looking at Bess. "Oh dear, I'm so sorry."

"It's not your fault," Bess said.

"The seltzer water will take that wine out of your sweater," Hannah said, nodding approval at Naomi. She took a napkin and began dabbing at Bess's sweater. "See, it's working already," she said. "Later we'll throw it in the wash, and it'll be good as new."

"Maybe I should go upstairs and change," Bess said, sounding doubtful.

Nancy instantly pulled back her chair. "I'll come with you. We can use the penlight to find our way up the stairs, and I can get the good flashlight I left in my room."

"I guess there's a storm somewhere. Happens a lot at home, too—electricity goes out," George remarked.

Nancy looked out the window. A full moon dangled over the alley of oaks along the drive. Except for moonlight, the grounds were dark. All the lamps along the walkways were out. Light twinkled in the houses nestled against the distant hills. "Looks like the storm hasn't really hit out there. It's pretty clear." She turned to Naomi. "The outage seems to be pretty localized."

Naomi followed Nancy's gaze. "Yeah, the weather didn't do this. Maybe someone hit an electrical pole or a tree, and the lines are down."

Just then there was the sound of something clinking on a glass. Mike's calming voice rose above the general din. "Everybody, there's nothing to worry about. The power's out, in case you haven't noticed," he added wryly. Laughter rippled around the room. Servers brought lit candles to the tables. The dining room slowly began to glow with dim light.

"The problem's the line leading in from the road, or wiring in the house. Please be patient and relax. The staff is getting candles. We have plenty of emergency lanterns for the resort guests, and flashlights to help the rest of you out to your cars." By now the room was bathed in candlelight. "Please, enjoy a cocktail on the house. If your dinners are delayed more than another five minutes, we'll give you all a raincheck to come back at your convenience for a free meal." Applause and a few cheers greeted Mike's announcement.

When Mike was finished, Nancy went upstairs with Bess. The landing between the first and second floor was dark, but the corridor leading to the west wing and their rooms was lit.

"Oh, the power's back on!" Bess said.

"I can skip the flashlight," Nancy said, following her toward her room.

"You don't have to stay," Bess told her. "I'll be down in a second. This means dinner will be on the table pretty soon."

Nancy left the room and headed to the stairs. When she rounded the corner she saw that the hallway that ran the length of the main building was dark. *Weird,* she thought, and hurried back to her room. After grabbing her flashlight, she knocked on Bess's door. "Here, you'll need this after all. Only *some* of the lights are back on." Nancy handed Bess her penlight. "I'm going downstairs. Mike should know there are lights on, at least in this part of the building."

Nancy reached the lobby and almost bumped right into Mike. He was holding a flashlight and heading for the kitchen. He was surprised to learn the upstairs lights were on.

"All I know is that the electrician finished upgrading the service just yesterday. None of the lights should be out. Just my luck," he grumbled. "I only hope that critic wasn't here tonight."

"Even if he or she were," Nancy soothed, "I'm sure the critic would understand. This could happen to anyone."

Mike patted Nancy's arm. "Unfortunately, not all the guests are as understanding as you."

Nancy knew that was all too true. She hoped that grumpy Monica Sanchez was in a minority of one.

"Jillian is trying to unruffle everyone's feathers. I do admire that woman's patience!" he said. "Fortunately she's the half of this duo who is better with people. It comes from her working all those years as a model. Lots of prima donnas in that field. I only wish she could clone herself and help me face Cadot."

"Do you mind if I come along?" Nancy asked Mike as he started down the hall. The kitchen had two other entrances besides the back door leading from the yard. One opened into a serving area that led directly to the dining room. The other smaller entrance was adjacent to the back stairs, in the hall.

"Sure, come along," Mike said. He squared his shoulders before walking into the kitchen.

"I'm afraid our chef of the month is beyond temperamental. Here goes nothing," he murmured.

The kitchen was ablaze with candlelight. Chef Cadot sat, arms folded, in front of the center counter. Several assistants were moving around the kitchen. Most of them looked like they would like to be far from the irate chef.

At Mike's entrance, a guy who had been lounging against one of the stainless-steel refrigerators straightened right up. Nancy saw his uniform had the name RYAN embroidered in red on the pocket. *Bess is right,* Nancy thought. *This guy's a serious hunk.* He walked toward Mike.

"This eeze it! I quit!" Monsieur Cadot threatened in a thick French accent.

"Now Louis, please be patient. We're working on the problem." Mike had adopted his soothing tone again.

"*Oui,* I know this. I am no fool! But I cannot work in a dark kitchen." He made a big show of looking at his watch.

Nancy noticed that though the lights were off, gas-fueled burners under various pots on the stoves were still lit. The aroma in the kitchen was wonderful. Part of her was dying to know exactly what was cooking. She hadn't had a chance to really study the menu before the lights went out.

"If the lights are not on in five minutes, dinner is finished for the evening. You order pizza for your guests. I stay one more day—then any more problems and I am finished, *finis! Comprendez-vous?* Do you understand me?"

"I'm sure this will be fixed in a minute. It's probably just an overloaded circuit. If the circuit breakers won't switch on, we'll call the electrician." Mike crossed the kitchen.

29

"Do you need help? I'm pretty handy," Ryan volunteered. "And I see we've got a couple of flashlights," he said, looking at the one Nancy was holding. "Can I borrow that?"

"Sure," she said, following him and Mike to the basement. It smelled a bit musty, but not unpleasant. Nancy guessed that it probably stretched beneath the whole big building. She wondered if it might even connect to that root cellar Jillian had told them about.

"Now where is that box?" Mike wondered. "I'm ashamed to admit I've only been down here a couple of times. When the electrician was here I was stuck up in Pittsfield dealing with the motor vehicles department."

"Over here!" Ryan said, leading the way around the back of the staircase.

"You seem to know your way around," Nancy observed as Ryan stopped at the back wall.

"I'm supposed to be Cadot's apprentice," he explained, "but since I'm pretty handy, Jillian sent me to help the electrician. I worked as a handyman to help pay for college."

Ryan handed Nancy the flashlight, and she aimed it at the wall. The beam illuminated three large gray metal electrical boxes. They were closed. Taped to the outside of each one was a printed sheet of paper with numbers and lines. Nancy recognized them from the small box of circuit breakers in her own basement back in River Heights. They indicated which breaker was connected to which area of the house. But the lines on these sheets were not filled in. "How come these are blank?" she asked.

"The electrician is coming back Monday to finish up the job," Mike explained. "He did the main work. He has to finish labeling things, and wanted to be sure power was adequate on each line so we wouldn't have a power outage. Guess he's going to have to rearrange things."

Nancy aimed her flashlight at the first box, but Ryan had already opened the middle box. At least fifteen breakers were inside, all unlabeled.

"Here's the problem," Ryan said, pointing to three heavy-duty plastic switches in the "off" position. He flipped each one. The first turned on the basement lights; when the last one snapped to the "on" position, a cheer could be heard above their heads, coming from the dining room. "Did it!" he announced proudly.

"You're a genius!" Mike said, thumping Ryan on the back.

"How'd you know it was the center box?" Nancy was impressed.

"Well, I worked with the guy yesterday. But I admit this was mostly a lucky guess. I vaguely remember him saying something about grouping each wing of the house together. And I've got a photographic memory, more or less," he said.

"Well, thank you," Mike said, hurrying back up the stairs. "You've saved the day!" At the top step he turned to Ryan. "You've only been here a week, and I know Monsieur Cadot was reluctant to take you on as an apprentice—but we clearly made a good decision hiring you." Mike rubbed his chin. "Now I have to mollify the guests. I'll offer free drinks and that pass for a free meal for the diners who had to suffer through this."

"A free meal?" Ryan said. "But why? They'll be able to eat tonight."

"Maybe, if they bothered to stay around. Developing good relations with your clientele is the A-number-one rule of the hospitality industry. Remember that, Ryan." With that, Mike hurried back to the dining room.

Nancy hesitated before following Mike. "Why didn't the chef want to hire you?" she asked Ryan. He seemed pleasant and pretty smart.

Ryan shrugged. "Because I'm a vegetarian, and his specialties . . . well, they aren't vegetables."

"So why work here then?" Nancy had some vegetarian friends who couldn't stand the sight of raw meat.

"Because I want to be a chef, and this place is attracting the best in the business. And there will be lots of different guest chefs here over the course of the year. Cadot's vegetable dishes are great! Just wish he'd stick to them," Ryan added.

He returned to the kitchen and Nancy made her way back to the dining room. Mike was busy handing rain checks to diners who had just come to the resort for dinner. Meanwhile Jillian had stationed herself at the buffet sideboard where the staff had brought in a tureen of soup and platters of sandwiches. "I hear Ryan saved the day," Jillian said as Nancy approached.

"He sure did." Nancy looked around. There was a line at the small coat check. "I'm surprised so many people are leaving."

"That's okay. We'll be organized in time for the seven thirty seating to go as planned. I hope you'll bear with us, Nancy. We're giving you soup and sandwiches tonight. Paying guests will have tonight's dinner deducted from their bill when they check out," she added.

"That's pretty generous," Nancy said, grabbing a chicken sandwich.

"Hannah and your friends took their food to the lounge. We've got a good fire going," Jillian said. "It's cozy in there. One of the servers will be around, seeing if you need something to drink or soup refills."

Nancy carried her food into the lounge. Hannah was near one of the fireplaces, sipping coffee and talking to some of the other guests. She smiled at Nancy and gestured across the room to where Bess and George were settled on the floor in front of another fireplace. Nancy joined them. "I see Hannah found some new friends," Nancy remarked, settling on the rug next to George.

"They ran into each other at the buffet table and got into this big-time debate over the merits of leeks versus shallots—whatever *they* are." George laughed, then took a bite of her sandwich.

"Shallots are what make this soup so incredible," Bess said, then glanced wistfully into her mug. "Unfortunately, in about a minute I finished every last drop. And I don't dare go for seconds. Chef Cadot's cream of mushroom soup has about a year's worth of calories!"

"You could jog it off tomorrow," George suggested.

"Speak for yourself," Bess said. "Tomorrow and every day this week you'll find me in the kitchen learning all I can from Cadot."

Nancy glanced up from her mug of soup. "Oh, I suppose it's just the cooking lessons you're interested in, and not that apprentice—what's his name?" She pretended to have forgotten. "Oh yes, Ryan! Ryan Logan."

Bess tossed a napkin at Nancy. "Okay, I admit it! But he *is* sweet, isn't he?"

"Not the word I would use exactly," Nancy said. "Sweet" did not describe Ryan. He had an edge to him Nancy actually found appealing and more than a little intriguing. "But he sure is handy. He found that broken circuit breaker in two seconds flat."

"Wow—a real Renaissance man!" George joked.

"Hmmm," Nancy mused. She put down her mug and leaned back on her elbows. She stared into the fire a moment, then turned to George.

"Uh-oh, Nancy has that look about her," George said to Bess.

"Nancy, all that happened is that the lights went out. There's nothing really weird about that."

"Yes, there is, Bess. The electrician just upgraded the service. I can't imagine that he put so much wattage on any one line that the circuits got overloaded."

George wrapped her arms around her knees and shrugged. "Maybe he's a crummy electrician . . . but anyway, that doesn't make it a mystery to solve, Nan. The chef was probably using too many appliances at once."

"No, he wasn't," Bess stated firmly. "At today's cooking class Monsieur Cadot said he never even uses a food processor. He's into doing everything by hand. He's very old-fashioned, and proud of it."

Nancy wondered what Hannah thought about that. As far as Nancy knew, Hannah adored the fancy food processor Carson had given her for Christmas last year. But before Nancy could give it another thought, she heard angry voices in the lobby.

"Now what?" George wondered as they all turned around to see what was happening.

35

"Is that a film crew?" Bess said, staring at the half dozen young men and women who were mobbing the registration desk. They were carrying all sorts of heavy cases.

"Mike never mentioned someone making a movie here!" Nancy said, scrambling to her feet for a better look.

Suddenly one voice rose above the others. "Look, I know we have no reservation." Nancy spotted a petite dark-haired woman standing at the desk. "I shouldn't need one. Mike will be more than happy to see me," she stated emphatically.

"Mr. Rinaldi?" A young woman behind the desk called for her manager. "We've got a problem here."

Mike hurried in from the dining room. He stared at the pile of luggage and the camera equipment, then spotted the woman. His dark complexion paled, and he looked anything but happy.

"What in the world are *you* doing here?" he asked.

4

Just Desserts

"Delighted to see you too," the woman snapped back. "I was in the neighborhood and thought it would be a good time to drop in to congratulate you on your success."

The woman's sarcasm seemed to roll right off Mike's back.

"Who exactly are all these people?" he asked, not bothering to hide his anger.

"My crew!" the woman said. As Nancy watched this exchange she suddenly recognized the woman. It had been years since she last saw her, but Nancy remembered the woman's sparkly eyes, thick dark hair, and pleasant voice.

"It's Lauren Rinaldi," she whispered to George.

"His ex?" Bess said, standing on tiptoe to see over

George's shoulder. "She's no Jillian Coatley, but she's awfully pretty," Bess remarked.

"Pretty or not, I don't get the impression she's welcome here," Nancy said. She moved closer to the lobby so she could hear what was going on.

"Smile, Mike. This is in the category of a good thing." Lauren gave an impatient snort. "We're filming a segment on wild game for our 'Harvest Holiday' show. I realized we were only a few miles from you. In case you forgot, you told me a little while ago that you loved the idea of Gourmet Getaway being featured on TV. I figured I'd kill two birds with one stone."

"The timing's a bit off, Lauren," Jillian said. She was standing next to Mike now, and looking a little sour. "We're short on rooms. Dinner's backed up. We've had a power outage—"

"And Cadot is throwing a temperamental fit in the kitchen," Mike added. "I can't afford to have a second dinner seating turn into another fiasco. I have to get back to the kitchen. I can't deal with this." He cast a pleading glance at Jillian.

Jillian took a deep breath. "You go back to Cadot," she said. Mike backed into the dining room.

"And don't worry," Lauren added quickly. "Look, my crew is young. They have camping equipment and can camp on the grounds, or spread out sleeping bags in one of the barns if you don't like the clutter of the tents on your lawn. If that's okay with you," she said to Jillian.

"Whatever you think will work." Jillian's cheerful tone sounded forced.

"And I can help in the kitchen. You know I'm a whiz at the chopping block!" Lauren said this a little too breezily.

Jillian stared a moment at Lauren, and her shoulders sagged slightly. Nancy knew from what Carson had told her that Jillian had helped Mike find backers to open the Getaway. Her modeling career had provided all the right connections. She had a natural grace with people, but she couldn't cook. "Good idea. Just let me go ahead and help Mike smooth the way for you. Cadot might resent you, though, for invading his domain."

"Believe me, I understand," Lauren said. "Cadot and I go way back—I used to produce his cooking show before I got my own gig. He's *beyond* touchy. Now while the crew gets settled for the night, maybe you and I can go over your lineup of cooking activities for the guests tomorrow. I'm sure there will be *something* interesting to film," she added.

"Anything for publicity," Jillian admitted, looking anything but pleased. With a sigh, she called Naomi and asked her to help Lauren's entourage set up quarters in one of the barns.

Nancy lingered long enough to watch the two

women disappear into the small office behind the registration desk to schedule the next day's shoot. Then she rejoined her friends, bringing them each sodas.

"So *that's* the ex-wife," Bess said, staring at the closed office door. "She's sure got some bad timing if she wants to film this place."

"Mike would agree with you there," Nancy said.

"Still she *is* doing him a favor—TV exposure will really draw crowds," George pointed out.

"And she did warn them about the food critic coming," Bess reminded them.

"Which means she knows who the critic is," Nancy said, her eyes brightening. "Let's see who Lauren spends time with tomorrow. Maybe that'll give us a clue about who the critic really is."

"And we can let Mike know. He could give the critic some extra perks."

"I doubt he'd do that—it would be a dead give-away he was trying to influence a review," Nancy said. "Still, I'm sure he'd like to know who it is."

Later that night Nancy was brushing her hair in front of the bedroom mirror when Hannah came out of the bathroom. Wrapped in a terrycloth robe, she rummaged in her suitcase, then dumped the contents of her large purse on the bed. Finally she looked up, puzzled. "Nancy, did you see my little cosmetic case— the blue one with the white flowers?" she asked.

"No, Hannah." Nancy put down her brush and checked the clutter of makeup, brochures, and packages on top of the dressing table. "Where did you see it last?"

"Let's see . . . I think in the airport. I freshened up in the ladies room before we picked up the rental car. My purse was feeling a bit heavy, so I thought I tucked it in that little carryall bag. But I must have left it in the car. Unfortunately my toothbrush was in it." Hannah sighed and went to the closet to retrieve her clothes.

"Don't you bother getting dressed again. I'm still in my jeans. I'll just put on a sweater and my shoes. It'll take a sec to get it. Besides, I could use a breath of air," Nancy said. She was still feeling a bit stuffed from her soup and sandwich and was dying to stretch her legs.

Nancy slipped into her moccasins, pulled on a sweater, grabbed a flashlight, and left the room. The wall sconces in the hall had been dimmed for the evening, but voices and soft laughter could be heard coming from the downstairs lounge.

She started for the front staircase, then thought to herself how that might be too conspicuous. Taking the back stairs would make more sense. She ran down the steps and out the door. Dried leaves rattled on the vine-covered wooden lattice to the right of the door.

She flicked on her flashlight and walked out to the van. After retrieving Hannah's bag, she started back for the hotel. Out of the corner of her eye she spotted two figures huddled against the side of the greenhouse. One was a bit taller than the other, and his hair glinted in the moonlight. *Hmm . . . could be Ryan,* Nancy thought, and she wondered who the girl was with him. They seemed to be talking in a rather agitated fashion. Suddenly Nancy felt like she was witnessing some private argument between a couple. Turning quickly, she hurried back onto the porch. She switched off her flashlight, opened the back door, and heard the sound of a woman's voice coming from just inside the kitchen. She could see that the door separating the kitchen from the hall was cracked open.

Nancy was about to go inside when she heard the woman say, "Gourmet Getaway has the potential of being the new hot thing in luxury resorts—*if* it makes it through the winter." The woman's laugh sounded almost cruel. "They already have some strikes against them."

There was a pause.

"Look, where are you anyway?" the woman sounded annoyed.

There was a pause, then the same voice spoke again. "I'll explain in person."

After another pause the woman said brusquely, "Look, we'll pull this off. I promise. And believe me, you won't regret it. Trust me. Gourmet Getaway will get exactly what it deserves!"

5

Market Madness

Exactly what it deserves? Now *that* sure sounded sinister. Nancy pressed her ear closer to the back door. As she leaned forward the porch floorboards let out a loud creak. Nancy grimaced in dismay.

"Hey, I've gotta go." The woman's voice dropped to a loud whisper, but Nancy could still hear. "Someone's here—I can't be caught talking with you." There was the snap of a cell phone being shut, then muffled footsteps approached the back door. Nancy ducked silently behind the vine-covered lattice and flattened herself against the wall.

The porch door creaked open. "Who's there?" the woman called. Through the vines Nancy couldn't see who she was, but she realized the woman probably couldn't see her, either. Nancy held her breath while the woman walked out to the top porch step. She surveyed the barnyard, looked around the porch, shrugged, then went back inside.

Nancy forced herself to stay put and not follow right away. She counted to twenty, then eased herself around the lattice. She cleared her throat, pulled out her flashlight, walked inside, and slammed the door behind her. In case the woman was still around, Nancy wanted to look as if she'd just returned from running her errand out to the car.

The softly lit back hall was empty, and so were the stairs. Had the woman already gone upstairs, or was she in the lounge? Nancy wasn't sure that she could recognize the woman simply by virtue of the shape she'd seen through the vines. She was about to check the lounge when Hannah appeared at the top of the back stairs.

"Nan? You okay?" Hannah called down the steps.

"Sure. I just wanted to stretch my legs a minute more," Nancy told Hannah, hurrying up the stairs. "And I found this," she said, brandishing the makeup case.

As they headed back toward their room Nancy asked, "By the way, did you see anyone in the hall just now?"

Hannah shook her head, then suddenly stopped right outside their room. She planted her hands on her hips. "Nancy Drew," she said, narrowing her eyes. "What are you up to? What's going on around here?"

Nancy playfully butted Hannah's shoulder as she passed her and entered the room. "What makes you ask?"

Hannah grinned but didn't answer. She didn't need to. Hannah had known Nancy too long and too well for the girl to try to fool her.

"Okay, I have no idea—at least not yet!" Nancy admitted and began to move toward her room.

It was only later, when she had turned out the lights and was lying in bed, that Nancy put two and two together. That woman had been talking on a cell phone—but Waringham was a dead zone.

The next morning Bess and George followed Hannah out the Getaway's front door, but Nancy started in the opposite direction. They all had signed on for Chef Cadot's shopping expedition into Waringham.

George wore only a thick gray Irish-knit sweater and a red scarf around her neck—she was always warm, no matter how cold it was outside. Hannah, on the other hand, was practically buried in this season's new style: a fake-fur coat.

"*Now* where are you going, Nancy?" Bess asked, pulling on a pair of pink mittens.

"Be there in a sec! I need to talk to Mike a minute," Nancy replied, pulling on her navy blue peacoat. Though she was eager to join her friends, Nancy still hadn't had a chance to talk to Mike about her encounter with Nate Caldwell.

"Just don't be late. I don't want to miss this chance to shop with Chef Cadot in town," Bess called after her.

Nancy found Mike in the front office at the computer. His door was open, but she tapped on the door frame before walking in. When he saw her, his expression shifted from worried to relieved.

"Nancy, come on in," he said. "Aren't you going on Chef Cadot's shopping tour?"

"Wouldn't miss it," Nancy said. "But I needed to talk to you."

"What's up?" Mike asked, leaning back in the old leather desk chair.

Nancy first told him about her encounter with Nate, then went on to describe the overheard phone conversation. As she spoke Mike looked increasingly concerned. "What I don't understand is how that woman used a cell phone. Isn't the whole area a dead zone?"

"Not the inn. The cell phone reception is good from here to about five miles north. Then it peters out again," Mike answered.

"Interesting. You know, I'm not sure that power outage was an accident last night. I don't know. I can't piece anything together at all. But Nate certainly seems to deeply resent, if not outright hate, this place and you guys. And to whom exactly was that woman talking?"

Mike heaved a sigh. "I have no idea about the woman, but what you heard certainly did sound a bit threatening. There have been some rumblings around here about 'Boston folk' barging in and overrunning the county with tourists who don't respect the land. And then there are the antihunting fanatics. . . ."

"I heard about them in town."

"They haven't really bothered us—not yet. I'm prepared to put up with whatever they do, though, as long as it's within the law. And as for Nate . . ." Mike seemed to choose his words carefully before going on. "He's difficult, Nancy, no doubt about that. And I'm troubled about that incident. But Caldwell was probably just aiming for that deer. He's a very good hunter, and it is the end of archery season, so he was within his rights to be hunting—"

"On *your* property?" Nancy was surprised.

"It's complicated. Nate kind of came with the place. He was the groundskeeper for the previous owners. The sales agreement and deed allow him lifetime rights to his old hunting cabin in the woods. He lives here, in a way. And though he's well known for being eccentric, I can't say he's caused any problems for us so far. I'll try to keep a closer eye on him.

"As for the phone call—I don't like the sound of that. Nancy, maybe you wouldn't mind keeping your eyes and ears open to see if you can find out what's going on."

"*If* anything's going on," Nancy added with a quick smile. "I *have* been accused of seeing mysteries where none exist."

Mike laughed. "Well, I hope that's the case this time round."

"One thing," Nancy concluded. "Please don't tell anyone—including Jillian—that I'm checking things out around here."

"Why not Jillian? She certainly has nothing to do with whatever's going on here."

"Of course not," Nancy hastened to reply, though her own experience had taught her never to rule out anyone as a suspect. Still, Jillian certainly had no motive to sabotage the resort she had helped start. "But it will make my job easier if no employees or guests know I'm investigating. Jillian might let something slip."

Reluctantly Mike agreed. As Nancy turned to leave he put a fatherly arm around her shoulders. "I know you enjoy your investigations, Nancy, but I hope you leave enough time to participate in our various activities here. The purpose of inviting you and your friends was for you to have a vacation—not to work!"

"Not to worry," Nancy assured him. "I already have the day planned. After shopping with the chef,

48

I'm going to his cooking class this afternoon. Then I'm going on Naomi's wild-food walk. I've always been interested in hunting mushrooms and finding wild roots and herbs."

Nancy hurried outside and climbed into the Getaway's minibus. Lauren's video camera man, a guy who'd introduced himself at breakfast as Dean Schultz, was already interviewing Chef Cadot in the seat behind the driver.

Sliding into the seat Bess had saved for her, Nancy whispered, "Cadot's a bit of a ham."

"The camera keeps him on his best behavior," George said wryly.

"Chef Cadot," Dean said as the minibus started up, "tell us exactly what this shopping expedition is about. We know the Gourmet Getaway has cooking classes for interested guests—but what does shopping have to do with cooking?"

Bess rolled her eyes at that question and gave Dean a thumbs-down sign.

Nancy barely restrained a giggle. It *was* a dumb question. Nancy wasn't much of a cook herself, but shopping for ingredients seemed a pretty important part of the process—as Chef Cadot himself began to explain.

"*Bon.* That eees a most excellent question. Every meal, you see, even the most simple meal, begins with the ingredients—what the careful cook selects in the store. *Par exemple,* today we shop for ingredients for tonight's wild-game specialty. . . ." The chef paused for effect, then added with a flourish of his hands, "Stuffed pheasant! Locally harvested of course."

"Then why go to the market?" Dean sounded confused.

"For zee truffles of course!" Cadot responded in his thickest accent.

George looked like she was about to gag. "Pheasant stuffed with chocolate?"

"No, George," Bess said. "These truffles aren't chocolate—they're mushrooms dug up by pigs in France!"

George still looked skeptical. "Can't say that sounds much better."

"You'll love them," Hannah spoke up from the seat behind the girls. "In fact, I used truffle oil on the last birthday pizza I made for you—and I seem to remember you ate half of it yourself."

"Oh." George looked surprised, and quickly humbled.

While the chef continued talking to the camera, Nancy looked around the minibus. It was full of mainly older couples and a few single men and women, all over age forty. A small contingent of Cadot's assistants, all closer to Nancy's age, were in the backseat laughing and joking among themselves. One assistant, she noticed, was missing.

"What happened to Ryan?" she whispered to Bess.

Bess's face fell. "When I saw him earlier, he told me he couldn't come. Something about waiting with Mike for the electrician. But personally, I think he's just camera shy. Would you believe it? He's been avoiding Lauren's crew like the plague."

When the small bus reached Waringham, the hamlet was anything *but* a ghost town. Almost every parking place was taken. People were walking in and out of the stores. The single pump at the gas station had a line of cars waiting to fill up.

"Now zees is one of the best features of the Getaway," Chef Cadot said as the driver parked the bus. "Zees Waringham market eees a surprising place. It is what Americans call a 'general store,' but it eees full of fine foods. It also has an excellent selection of truffles and dried mushrooms—as good as I have found at any gourmet store in Boston."

"The food isn't the only surprise," George said as everyone climbed out of the bus.

Nancy followed George's gaze. Two groups of picketers were parading outside the Waringham store. A state trooper was standing in front of the group, to the left of the store's entrance; the second group of demonstrators was kept in check by a man wearing a jacket with the word SHERIFF emblazoned on the back.

"Now what is this about?" Hannah said, turning up the collar of her fake-fur jacket.

Nancy read the signs quickly. "Seems to be an

animal rights group over there on the left," she said.

"And a prohunting contingent on the right," George pointed out. "I've never seen hunters protesting anything before."

"I guess the antihunting crowd is getting a bit more aggressive around here," Nancy replied.

"Are we still going in?" Bess looked hesitant. "I mean, crossing a picket line is scary."

"It's not that kind of picket line. Each group is just trying to make a point," Hannah assured her. "Whatever these people are arguing about isn't any real concern of ours. We don't hunt, and seldom do I eat game—unless it's an occasion like this trip to the Getaway."

Chef Cadot seemed oblivious of the demonstrators. He led the way toward the entrance to the store, talking to his class. Nancy could see he was still performing for the video camera—but Dean had turned the camera away from the celebrity chef and trained it on the two groups of protesters. As the shoppers neared the store entrance, both groups increased the volume of their shouts.

"Animals have rights too!" shouted the animal-rights contingent. They were a large ragtag bunch. Most jabbed picket signs into the air: SAVE THE ENVIRONMENT. STOP ANIMAL MURDER NOW! Some members of the group held banners announcing they were from local chapters of national vegetarian and animal rights organizations that were familiar to Nancy.

The smaller prohunting group held homemade signs reading ANIMAL CONTROL SAVES FORESTS and RESPONSIBLE HUNTING FEEDS FAMILIES. A few of the more vocal members responded to the animal rights chants by shouting, "Save the trees, cull the deer!"

"Nancy, look who's there." George pointed to the prohunting group.

It was Nate Caldwell. Nancy wasn't surprised. Just seeing him jab a homemade prohunting sign in the air made her mad. "Too bad he doesn't just confine his hunting to wild game," she grumbled as they continued toward the store.

Dean had motioned for another member of the crew to join him. They jogged up to the demonstrators and began interviewing a woman who seemed to be the leader of the animal rights group.

"Nancy, look!" Bess said, grabbing Nancy's arm. "Isn't that Ryan?"

Nancy followed the direction of Bess's gaze. Ryan's mop of blond hair was easily detectable, even at the back of the animal rights crowd. "He's a vegetarian. I guess he just wanted to register his protest," Nancy said, thinking the young man hadn't been camera shy after all. He probably didn't want to be seen by his animal rights buddies climbing out of the Gourmet Getaway minibus.

Maybe they didn't even know he worked at the resort.

"What did you say?" Chef Cadot had fallen in step with Nancy and Bess. "You saw Ryan somewhere?" They were climbing the three shallow steps leading to the porch of the general store. "I have not been able to find him. He was supposed to come with us here—I was going to teach him about the mushrooms and truffles. Sometimes I want to feed zeez vegetarians lots of red meat. They—how do you say it?—are 'space people.'"

"Space cadets," Bess said with a giggle. Nancy turned to point to where she had last seen Ryan. "Looks like he's vanished."

The words were scarcely out of her mouth when something flew straight at the chef's head. "Watch out!" Nancy shouted. At the same instant, a voice cried out, "Cadot's a murderer!" A handful of stones flew past Nancy's shoulder.

The state trooper hurried to the Getaway group. "Inside the shop . . . now!" he commanded, and half shoved Nancy and the chef into the store. The owner was already at the door as the rest of the Getaway's small crowd practically tumbled in behind the trooper.

"What happened?" the shopkeeper cried, visibly shaken. He pulled off his apron and rushed over to Nancy.

54

"I think that protest just got out of hand," the trooper said. "I'm going to break this up now. Peaceful protest is one thing. Stone throwing is not our way around here." He started for the door, then turned to Nancy. "Are you okay?"

"I'll be fine," Nancy said, feeling both embarrassed and hopping mad.

"Did you see who did this?" the trooper asked. Nancy read his name tag above his badge: TROOPER WILLIAM DONLEVY.

"No, Officer Donlevy," she said, then turned to George. "How about you?"

George shook her head. "To tell you the truth, I'm not sure it even came from one of the animal rights people. Some of the prohunting guys were hanging out next to the animal rights folk, and they were arguing or something."

Hearing that, Nancy grew thoughtful. Where had Nate Caldwell been when those stones were thrown? Had he slipped behind the animal rights group? Maybe he shouted "murderer" at the chef to deflect attention from himself, and his real target, her. Or maybe she was jumping to conclusions.

"Yes, I saw that," Trooper Donlevy said. "I'm going out there now and putting a stop to this nonsense."

One of the store's employees led Nancy to the rest room to help her freshen up. Nancy's mood wouldn't heal so quickly. She couldn't believe that someone had actually tried to throw stones at the chef. When she returned to the front of the store, the owner, who introduced himself to her as "Matt," handed her a box of chocolates along with his apologies.

"I can't believe this happened on the doorstep of my store. I don't argue with a person's right to protest and have different opinions, but this is vandalism. And Monsieur Cadot, I'm mortified. Obviously those stones were aimed at you. Here, take this as a gift—and I hope you won't hold this against us. Gourmet Getaway is a very important customer." With that, Matt handed the chef a large cellophane bag full of truffles.

The chef's eyes opened wide with amazement. "Zees, Monsieur Matt, is too generous," he said, and Nancy could see he meant it. She didn't know much about truffles, except that they fetched a high price and were considered a great delicacy.

"And take these, too," Matt said, hurrying over to a row of plastic bins. He opened one and scooped out a large quantity of dried mushrooms. "Morels. These are local—dried by one of our local mushroom hunters."

"Zees must weigh half a pound!" The chef beamed, then pumped Matt's hand. "Zees is too generous. You will be my guest for a meal at the Getaway before I leave next month, yes?"

"Yes!" Matt replied heartily. "Now what can I do for you—that is, if you're still in the mood to give your shopping tour?"

Cadot nodded and led the group down the first aisle. It was filled with bottles of expensive and unusual olive and nut oils.

"Nancy," George said, touching her friend's sleeve to stop her. "Look at this."

She handed Nancy a flier. "Hmm . . . a conflict resolution meeting to help ease the tensions between the animal rights groups, the hunters, and the local businesses. Now *that* seems useful, considering the mood of that crowd out there."

"It's tonight, in the town hall. Let's go, Nancy," George said.

"Do we have to?" Bess groaned, hearing what her friends were saying. "It sounds boring, and Chef Cadot is holding a special dessert class. Hannah and I were planning to attend. Jillian said the class will be followed by a chocolate tasting!"

"Now that's a tough choice," Nancy said. "But I really want to check out the meeting at the town hall. You and Hannah should go to the class."

"And save some of that dessert for us!" George begged.

All at once there was the sound of something shaking, then the whole shelf fixture in front of them began to sway.

"The shelf!" George warned. "It's falling. . . ."

Nancy watched in horror as the tall shelving unit wobbled and teetered. Her hand shot out to grab one end of it. Matt was nearby and grabbed the other, but not before several bottles and jars showered down on top of the chef.

6

A Walk on the Wild Side

There was a stunned silence. A last can rolled off the shelf and rattled down the aisle toward the back of the store. The noise propelled everyone into action. Several people rushed up to help right the heavy shelving unit.

"Chef Cadot!" Nancy cried, rushing to the chef's side. He sat against a display case, staring in horror at his hands. His right hand was bleeding. Careful to avoid the glass, Nancy stooped down and touched his arm. "Are you okay?"

"What happened?" His face was pale. Nancy saw that he was in shock.

Matt grabbed the phone on the counter and dialed 911 for the paramedics. Someone else called in the trooper from outside.

Hannah found towels and ice. Within minutes the chef had been seated in a chair, his right hand was wrapped in a towel, and the bleeding was stanched. Though he still looked shaken, Matt called his stock boys to sweep up the glass and mop up the mess on the floor.

"Now *this* is going way too far." Officer Donlevy took in the scene with obvious disgust. "This is serious vandalism plus attempted assault. Matt, you should file a police report."

"I will. I'll come to your office later," the storekeeper said.

The officer asked people in the store, "Did anyone see anything or anyone suspicious?"

Several noes rose up from the small crowd. Matt shepherded the Gourmet Getaway group toward the counter, and one of his clerks poured complimentary hot cider.

"I'll check the videotape," Dean volunteered, pressing the playback button. Nancy peered over his shoulder. The video screen zoomed to Cadot pointing to one of the shelves. The angle was too narrow to see behind the shelving unit.

"Nothing here," Nancy said. "But someone certainly could have been hiding back there, given the shelf a quick shove, then vanished." In the commotion, the culprit could have easily slipped out of the store, or melted into the crowd of customers.

"And since someone just hurled a stone at Cadot and called him a murderer," Officer Donlevy pointed out, "I doubt this was an accident. It's too much of a coincidence." The wail of a siren outside the store heralded the arrival of the ambulance and rescue squad.

"No hospital!" the chef protested rather weakly.

"Yes, you have to go to the hospital," Officer Donlevy insisted as the paramedics hurried into the store. "You probably need stitches. I'd think, since you're a chef, you'd want to make sure that hand heals up right."

"This is not exactly what I had in mind when I signed up for the cooking class," Bess murmured. Several hours had passed since the incident in the store. Nancy cast a sympathetic smile across the counter in the Getaway's kitchen. Smothered in a big white apron, with a chef's hat perched on top of her blond hair, Bess was looking a bit queasy. The class was in the process of "dressing" pheasants.

Nancy had been surprised to learn that dressing the pheasant meant cleaning the bird, not stuffing it. Under the close supervision of Chef Cadot, and with the help of the chef's apprentices, each student was involved in the preparation. With obvious distaste Ryan was finishing plucking the last feathers from that night's dinner. Nancy watched his complexion turn pale green, like Bess's. Nancy felt sorry for Ryan. Like Bess, the vegetarian hadn't quite signed on for this experience. But unlike Bess, he couldn't hang back.

Dean, Lauren, and the video crew, on the other hand, were loving every minute of the class. Especially since the chef was in a mood. Infuriated by the bulky bandages on his right hand, he was ordering his helpers around like a drill sergeant. He was only a degree more congenial to his class of Getaway guests. One or two had already slipped out of the kitchen.

Hovering near the counter, Mike watched the performance with dismay. What might make dramatic, or even humorous, video footage would certainly present a very bad picture of his resort.

"You, Ryan," Cadot bellowed, waving his right hand then wincing with pain. "Take the feathers outside. Go right to the Dumpster. We do not want to draw the attention of the raccoons to the back porch."

With visible distaste Ryan shoved the feathers into a garbage bag, peeled off the thin latex gloves he had been wearing, and added them to the bag before banging out the back door. Nancy could hear him stomp across the porch and clatter down the steps. He wasn't just upset, he was mad. Nancy didn't blame him. Cadot was forcing him to do work that was against his personal beliefs. Nancy wondered if he would bother to return.

"This is a sheer waste of time," Monica said. "I

hate all this mess!" she declared, casting a cold glance at the prep table. "I don't mind observing all of this, but I think I've helped enough for someone supposed to be on vacation." She untied her apron and tossed it on a stool. "I'm going to the office to ask Jillian if I can book a trail ride this afternoon."

"That is not a good attitude, Mademoiselle Sanchez!" Cadot remarked darkly.

The woman just shrugged and headed for the door, smoothing her long dark hair. Nancy couldn't believe how much the woman fussed with her hair. She had even refused to put on the regulation chef's hat. Nancy had suspected at first it was to avoid having to handle the food. Monica had made it abundantly clear that while she enjoyed *eating* gourmet food, the cooking should be left to someone else. Now Nancy figured she'd rejected the hat because she didn't want to mess her hair.

"Sorry to offend you, Monsieur Cadot," Monica retorted snidely from the doorway. "But it was my understanding that guests here are free to do what they want—and I don't want to be one of your kitchen lackeys!"

Dean deftly switched the camera from Monica to Cadot. Mike instantly positioned himself between the chef and the lens just as Cadot roared, *"Lackeys?* Zeez apprentices are here because they consider it an honor to work in my kitchen!"

"And," Mike interrupted quickly, "Ms. Sanchez has every right to go riding if that's her preference. I'm sure she meant no insult, Louis." Mike's tone was firm. "And I think maybe you are in too much pain to continue today."

"You cannot be serious!" Cadot jutted out his chin. "I will not leave my kitchen."

"Louis, it's only for a day or two. I think you'd better rest up. Didn't the doctors tell you not to use your hand?"

"I am not using my hand, Monsieur Rinaldi!" Cadot bristled. "I am using zees!" He tapped his forehead with the fingers of his left hand.

"And you will continue to use your head—*planning* the meals. But I want you to go to your cottage and stay there for the next two days," Mike said in a no-nonsense tone.

"And who exactly will do the cooking? Or supervise the apprentices?"

"I will!" Lauren volunteered instantly. The chef regarded Lauren for a moment, then heaved a big sigh. "Don't forget," Lauren added quickly, "you're still planning the meals. I'll supervise shopping and get them cooked. Meanwhile I'll call in the sous-chefs from the Laurel Lodge. They're closed for the season. Janice and Raoul could use a night's work."

"Go, Louis. Get some rest," Mike urged, gently guiding the man to the door.

Cadot took off his hat and apron, handed them to one of the helpers to put in the laundry, and went out the back door without further comment. From the kitchen window, Nancy watched the chef go onto the porch. He stopped and muttered to himself, then picked up a garbage bag from the steps. It was full of feathers, Nancy could tell from the way the chef effortlessly hoisted up the bag. In defiance or dis-taste—Nancy didn't know which—Ryan had left the sack on the porch steps.

The chef walked over to the Dumpster. After an awkward maneuver using his one good hand, he opened it and placed the bag inside. He turned and was walking toward his cottage when Nancy heard Lauren's voice addressing the class.

"Well, I guess the ball is in my court now!" Lauren said, sounding faintly smug. Nancy was startled by the sound of Lauren's voice. Nancy couldn't be sure, but it was awfully similar to the voice she'd over-heard on the phone the night before.

Lauren picked up just where Cadot had left off, moving into the role easily, as if she were born to teach cooking classes. "So now the nasty part is over—it's time to think about exactly how to go about cooking these pheasants. Chef Cadot's recipe calls for . . ."

Nancy tuned out the details of the recipe and found herself wondering. If it had been Lauren on the phone last night, what possible motive could she have to cause trouble for the Getaway? Was she *that* jealous that Mike and Jillian had made her own dream come true?

Halfway through the cooking class Nancy and George left to join Naomi's wild-food walk. Last night when she'd read over the Getaway's brochure, Nancy had been impressed to learn that Naomi not only had a degree in botany from a major university, but also specialized in wild edible plants and mushrooms.

After a quick tour of the herb garden, Naomi led the group into the woods. "If everyone gathers around this tree, I'll show you something *really* great." Naomi carefully put down the wicker basket she was carrying. Already it contained a surprising number of edible roots and herbs that had survived the frost. Only four guests had gone on the wild-food walk: They were joined by a man named Joe, and, to Nancy's amazement, Monica. She missed the first part of the walk, but turned up in the woods dressed in riding clothes and seemed extremely interested in the wild-food part of Naomi's tour. "Does anyone know what kind of tree this is?" Naomi asked.

"An oak," George answered instantly. George had won a merit badge in tree identification when she was a Scout in grade school.

Naomi looked surprised and pleased at George's answer. "Right," she said.

"So what if it *is* an oak?" Monica asked.

Naomi crouched down and pointed to a yellow-orange fungus that jutted out from the tree. "That's a good question, and I'll answer it later—but for now, take a look. Here's a mushroom that can provide a vegetarian with a dinner that tastes exactly like chicken." She looked at the group and seemed to relish their reactions.

"No way!" George exclaimed.

"I kid you not!" Naomi said, taking a sharp knife out of her basket. "You see, if you know what you're doing you can live off wild-vegetable food."

Nancy regarded Naomi more carefully. "Are you a vegetarian, like Ryan?"

Naomi frowned. "No, I'm not like Ryan. He's a vegan. He doesn't eat anything from animals: no dairy products, no eggs. It's too extreme for me. I eat cheese and eggs. Now watch how I do this," she said, gently cutting off a good portion of the mushroom. Nancy filed away that information about Ryan. It certainly explained why he, and not Naomi, was at the animal rights demonstration earlier in the day.

As she watched Naomi harvest the mushroom, Nancy was impressed by how careful she was not to cut the tree bark. "Now, when I gather it," Naomi told them, "I leave some behind to be sure the fungus continues to grow here." While she talked she wrapped the mushroom carefully in waxed paper before putting it in her basket. "It's a good practice to keep different kinds of wild mushrooms separate from each other, and to study them before you start preparing them for cooking. Anyone know why?"

"Because some are poisonous," Monica answered immediately.

"Right," Naomi said.

"How do you know which mushrooms are dangerous?" Nancy wondered.

"Experience, a lot of study, and learning to look carefully at anything you pick in the wild. It's useful to work alongside an experienced mushroom gatherer for a few seasons."

"But don't some poison mushrooms look exactly like ones that aren't?" Nancy inquired.

"Not exactly—but the differences are small, and a person has to be very focused to notice them. Remember how I told you that it's important to know this is an oak?" Naomi asked, standing up and brushing the dust off her hands. When people nodded, she turned and surveyed the area. Then she continued.

"That's because this same mushroom, when it grows on a different kind of tree or tree stump, might make you sick. It won't kill you, in this case, but you would be pretty unhappy if you ate it." She pointed to another mushroom. "Here's a chicken of the woods, and it's growing on the stump of a hem-lock. That's a conifer, and this particular mushroom is *not* edible when it grows on conifers."

"That's pretty tricky," George remarked.

Naomi checked her watch. "We've got to be get-ting back," she said. "This mushroom can be added to the mélange the chef planned as one of the side dishes at dinner."

As they went back to the path a figure came bar-reling down the trail. Nancy's stomach clenched. She recognized the man instantly. It was Nate. He was carrying an ax in one hand and a small bundle of kin-dling in the other. Nancy recoiled from the sight of him and his ax. The ax head was stained with some-thing red.

As the group parted to let him through he noticed Naomi's basket.

"Rabbit food!" He grunted, then laughed scorn-fully. "You people are crazy trying to live on that stuff. Me," he said, poking his own chest with the short handle of the ax, "I prefer the rabbit that I just pulled from the trap about an hour ago."

"You're disgusting. Has anyone ever told you that?" Naomi snapped.

"Because I have the courage to look what I eat in the eye while it's still alive?" Nate shot back. "We've all got our principles, you know." With that, he con-tinued his trek down the path.

"I can't believe Mike tolerates him," Naomi grumbled as they crossed the barnyard.

"Because he's a hunter?" Monica's voice held a challenge.

"That, too!" Naomi glared at Monica.

Nancy was surprised at the interchange. Monica had until now seemed generally bored with the whole Getaway scene. Nancy hadn't expected her to have opinions one way or another about hunting, or about food in general—except when it came to eating it.

Before she could give it another thought, George exclaimed, "Would you look at that?" She pointed toward the small cottage nestled in a grove of pines just beyond the kitchen garden.

"Chef Cadot's place," Naomi said. She sniffed the air and made a face. "He's cooking."

Nancy thought the air smelled wonderful. "Chicken soup." She identified the aroma instantly. "Even bandaged and banished from the Getaway kitchen, he can't stop himself from whipping up a meal."

"Naomi," Joe said. "What's that stuff hanging from the rafters of Cadot's porch?"

"Herbs we gathered from the garden. Of course we picked and dried them during the summer, before the frost—way before Cadot arrived last week," Naomi said. "Do you want to take a closer look?"

"I'd love it," Joe said.

"I'll pass," Monica announced. "I just took your

70

tour to kill time before I went riding, and I've got to get to the stables now. Jillian's waiting. We've got a date to go riding together. Ta." As Jillian approached, Nancy could see that her smile looked forced.

"Guess catering to difficult guests comes with owning a place like this," George murmured to Nancy.

"Can't say I envy Jillian right now," Nancy whispered as they followed toward the chef's front porch.

Approaching the cottage, George chuckled. "Look, he even has herbs decorating his door!"

Nancy followed the direction of George's gaze. What looked like a bunch of brown weeds was tacked to the chef's front door.

"Where did that come from?" Naomi said. She climbed onto the porch to take a closer look. Nancy was right behind her. As Nancy neared the door she peered over Naomi's shoulder. The weeds were oozing something sticky, bright, and bloodred.

And scrawled across Cadot's door was a single glistening word:

MURDERER

7

In the Soup

"Those aren't weeds," Naomi gasped, recoiling from the door. "They're feathers!"

They were pheasant feathers, like the ones they'd plucked in the kitchen; Nancy could see that now for herself. She took a closer look at the word scrawled on the door, then reached out to touch the red liquid.

"*Don't!*" Naomi warned, backing away from the pool of red fluid on the wood floorboards in front of Cadot's door. She pulled Nancy's hand away. "This is too much!" she said, and ran down the porch steps.

"Naomi, it's not blood!" Nancy called after her. "It's just paint." Naomi only shook her head, though, and continued running toward the inn's back door.

"It's still *beyond* gross." George sounded shaken. "Someone wanted us to *think* it was blood."

72

"This message wasn't meant for us," Joe said. "Someone is threatening Chef Cadot. We should definitely let Mr. Rinaldi know."

Before Nancy could respond, the chef's front door burst open. He had an apron tied around his middle, and was brandishing a wooden spoon in his good hand. "What is zee meaning of this? I am banished from my kitchen, ordered to rest, and then all this noise! Peace and quiet. Eeez zees too much to ask?" The next words died on his lips. "What eeez zees mess?" His cheeks burned with anger as his eyes traveled from the sloppily tied bouquet of pheasant feathers to the red paint.

When he spotted the word "murderer" painted on his door, the blood drained from his face. "Zees eeez—how do you say it?—the last straw! I am finished with zees place. Someone eeez out to ruin me. To destroy my reputation! I quit." Muttering in French, Cadot stormed toward the back kitchen door of the hotel, still clutching the wooden spoon in his good hand.

"Mike's going to have his hands full now," Nancy murmured.

"I hope Cadot doesn't really quit. I booked our stay here this week only because of him," Joe lamented, then looked down at Naomi's basket. It was lying on its side and the contents had scattered across the porch. "Maybe we should throw this stuff out."

"Why?" George said. She bent down, and started picking up the mushrooms, roots, and herbs they had gathered. "They didn't get into the paint, and they're no dirtier than they were when we picked them."

"I'll help you in a minute," Nancy promised. She had noticed a second puddle of paint to the left of the door. Someone had stepped in it, and a trail of increasingly faint red footprints led toward the side of the porch. "I want to check on something," she said, carefully following the trail. It led to the railing. The vandal had jumped over the railing—wearing gloves, Nancy realized. There were no red fingerprints on the railing. When Nancy climbed over the rail herself, she saw that the footprints gradually vanished in the dried grass. She retraced her steps back up to the porch, and knelt down to get a closer look at one of the prints. It was smeared; shreds of brown leaves, grass, and mud stuck to the paint. Checking the bottom of her own sneaker, she compared its tread with the marks made by the vandal's shoe. The treads didn't match at all. She was pretty sure the vandal wasn't wearing sneakers.

She was still studying the floorboards when George walked up. "Joe brought the basket back to the kitchen," George said, then noticed the footprints. "Can you tell anything from these?"

Nancy got up. "Only that whoever did this had big

74

feet. It was probably a guy, though I can't be sure. And he or she wasn't wearing sneakers."

"Nate wasn't wearing sneakers, and I'm sure you noticed his ax," George said quietly.

"I did. It had something red on it. And he *did* come from this direction when he ran into us just now."

"And Nan—he sure seems to have every motive to see this place fail."

Nancy stood up, swept her hair off her face, and stared in the direction of the forest. Did he, really? After all, he had lifetime rights to that cabin Mike told her about. Plus he could hunt on the grounds, which bordered state game preserves. Would a new owner of the resort be bound to keep him on? Nancy would have to check with her dad on that point. "I'm not sure he's the only one," Nancy said after a moment. "There are some other people who might want to see this place fail—or at least get a bad review this weekend."

"Right—if that critic is really here," George said, raking her fingers through her short dark hair. "But then, even if he or she missed that outage the other night, there's no way the critic hasn't at least heard of all the other disasters by now."

"George, why don't you hang around the inn in case anything else goes wrong. Keep an eye on things; pay attention to who's around, and who's not. I need to find Mike."

George returned to the inn while Nancy checked

the door more carefully. The writing was messy. Whoever had scrawled the word had been in a rush. On closer inspection Nancy saw the feathers weren't tied together with string, but duct tape. More tape secured them to the door.

Halfway across the yard Nancy ran into Ryan. He wasn't wearing an apron or a jacket. He was carrying a brown paper bag and looked cold.

"Hey!" he greeted her. He seemed in a rush and didn't bother to stop.

"You must be freezing," Nancy said as they passed each other.

"Yeah—well, I won't be out here long," he said, continuing to cross the yard. He smiled over his shoulder. "Gotta get ahold of Cadot. Lauren wants me to check a recipe."

Nancy stopped. "Didn't you hear?"

"Hear what?" Ryan stopped as well, and took a couple of steps toward Nancy.

"About Monsieur Cadot. Wasn't he in the kitchen just now? Looking for Mike?"

"Nope. Haven't seen either of them. That's why I have to check the recipe. What's going on?"

The wind was starting up and the sun was hanging low behind the hills. In spite of her jacket Nancy was cold. "Well, you can't check the recipe, Ryan. I mean, he's not at the cottage. He went to find Mike—he's about to quit."

"*Quit?*" Ryan repeated, shocked. "He can't quit! That'll hurt business, and if Mike doesn't do well this winter, I won't have a job. I *need* this job," he declared fiercely.

Nancy felt sorry for the guy, though after what Naomi told her, she was surprised he'd want to continue working in a place that served meat. He looked so genuinely upset, though, that she took pity on him. "Hey, Ryan," she said, touching his arm. "Don't worry. Mike will probably smooth things over. He's good at that."

"So far. But Cadot's got his pride, you know. And jobs are scarce here once the holidays are over."

Nancy couldn't argue with that. Suddenly she remembered Ryan's reaction to having to dispose of the pheasant feathers. "If I were you, I'd avoid the chef's cabin."

"Why?"

"It's a mess."

Ryan didn't ask any more. "Thanks for the heads up."

She glanced down and noticed Ryan's sneakers. The laces were untied. "You're going to trip on those laces."

Ryan looked at his feet, then flashed Nancy a smile. "I was in a rush to get out here. Guess I forgot to tie them." He stooped down, tied his shoes, then showed Nancy the paper bag in his hand. "Have to do my kitchen lackey thing; dump this in the garbage," he said. "See you back inside. Good luck finding Mike."

When Nancy got to the kitchen, Mike wasn't there. Several kitchen workers were attending to dinner. Jillian, who was poring over the menu, was still dressed for riding.

"I don't know where Mike is," Jillian told Nancy. She sounded remarkably calm for someone whose chef had just quit.

"That was a short trail ride," Nancy commented, feeling slightly puzzled.

"Too cold, and"—Jillian looked around and dropped her voice—"frankly, I was glad to be saved by my beeper. Lauren got a call and had to go off with her crew, so Mike needed me in the kitchen. It saved me from having to go on a trail with Monica. She laid a guilt trip on me in the office earlier about this being the worst vacation she's ever had. So in the interest of soothing an unhappy guest, I agreed to go riding with her."

"Did you hear about Cadot?"

"Hear about him?" Jillian smiled. "I heard *from* him. He came storming through here a little while ago. My French is rusty, but he was mumbling some-thing about the whole world wanting to murder him. He *did* say—in English—that he was looking for Mike, who conveniently seems to have disappeared. I think he's had enough fireworks for one day."

Jillian made a note on the master menu for the evening and handed it to one of the assistants. "Make these changes, and then print out the menus," she told him, and turned back to Nancy. "So, what is this about Cadot? He wouldn't talk to me. What's he so upset about now?"

Nancy debated with herself only a second. Better let Mike handle the chef. No point upsetting Jillian at this point. "Oh, there was a bit of a scene out by his cottage. He's miffed," was all she said.

"Well, we needed some fresh eggs for dessert, so Mike might be in the chicken house. I told Cadot the same thing."

Nancy thanked Jillian, zipped her jacket, and went back outside. The chicken house lay between the riding stables and the barn where the resort stored farm equipment, hay, and some of the groundskeeper's supplies. As she passed the barn Chef Cadot came stalking out. Through the open barn door Nancy caught a glimpse of the tents pitched by Lauren's crew. One of the women waved at Nancy just as the door slid shut behind Cadot.

At the sight of Nancy the chef's expression soured. "Oh, it's only you!" he exclaimed. "Where's Mike?" His tone was accusing. *Maybe he thinks I'm hiding him somewhere,* Nancy thought. Part of Nancy wanted to just ignore him. The man was so pompous! She almost laughed. He still held his wooden spoon, and his face was red—now not from anger, but from the cold.

"I'm looking for Mike too," Nancy said. "Have you tried the chicken house?"

The chef didn't answer. He marched past Nancy. They both spotted Mike at the same time. He was latching the door of the chicken coop.

"Rinaldi!" Cadot fumed. "I am finished with zees place. You fix your own dinners for the rest of the month. I leave as soon as I find a driver to take me to Boston. I cannot drive like zees." He waved his injured hand in the air. "And I will not risk my life to cook for zees rabble!"

"Risk your life?"

Nancy had to admire Mike. He calmly picked up the eggs in one hand and firmly gripped Cadot's arm in the other. "Now *that's* a bit extreme."

Cadot surprised Nancy by turning to her. "Tell him. You saw it!"

"Saw what, Nancy? What happened this time?" Mike asked, guiding them toward the riding stable. "It's warmer in here," he said. The place smelled of horses and clean hay, and it felt almost cozy.

Something moved in the back of the barn. Nancy tensed up. "Just horses in the stall," Mike assured them. Putting down the eggs, he sat on a bale of hay. "What's up?" he asked Nancy.

"Things are going from bad to worse, fast." She told Mike about the pheasant feathers, the bloodred paint, and the footprints on the cottage porch.

Mike listened with a grave expression while the chef knit his brow and studied Nancy's face.

"You sound like some kind of spy policeman—how do you say it here?"

Before Nancy could answer, Mike spoke up. "Louis, Nancy is not just a guest here. She's helping me discover who is behind the incidents we've had lately. There were a few earlier in the fall—maybe as far back as July, come to think of it. Things I chalked up to kids' pranks: garbage being strewn over the driveway at night, the mailbox being stolen."

"But now the vandalism's hit a whole new level," Nancy added. "The police were pretty upset by what happened in the store earlier today. They're starting to investigate on their own."

Mike ran his hand across his bald head. "Just the kind of publicity we *don't* need. I can see the head-lines now: *'Gourmet Resort with New Theme: Murder on the Menu!'*"

"Bad for business," Cadot agreed. "It could ruin you." He turned to Nancy. "You are not police. But you think you can find out what happens here?"

Nancy smiled ruefully. "I'll do my best. I guess I have a knack for this sort of thing."

Cadot grew thoughtful. "That would be good, Mike. No police. No publicity. Okay, I stay. Unless things become worse."

81

With that, Cadot huffed off. Mike took his cell phone and called the house, instructing some of the staff to clean up Cadot's porch.

Nancy waited until he hung up to tell him about the other clues she'd found, including Nate's ax. "I don't want to jump to conclusions," she added. "What would Nate have against Cadot anyway?"

"Nothing. But all the bad publicity, especially if we have to call the cops in on this, might do us in, Nancy. No one will want to stay in a resort with this kind of stuff going on."

"True. Can you think of anyone else who wants to see you fail?"

Mike threw up his hands and actually laughed. "Half the county—like I told you yesterday. And now protestors are picketing outside our gates. It's bad for business."

"Maybe the chef is the target, not the resort," Nancy mused. "We shouldn't rule that out."

Mike made a face. "I doubt it. The man is pompous, egotistical, and, like any chef of his caliber, has made enemies in the business. But I can't imagine another chef trying to wreck Cadot's reputation here. This is a small-time gig. Do you have any other ideas?"

Nancy hesitated. She was reluctant to mention her suspicions of Lauren, and the possibility that she was the person on the cell phone the night before. "Not firm ones. I've got to follow up on a couple of things, Mike. I'll let you know when I've got more concrete evidence. In the meantime, we should keep an eye on Nate—just in case."

Later that evening, after dressing for dinner, Nancy slipped out to the stables. She had decided to call her father and ask him about Lauren and Mike, and she wanted to keep her conversation private.

The night was turning bitter, and the cold seemed to pierce right through Nancy's jacket. Her blue dress was a light jersey, with long sleeves and a soft skirt that came just to her knees—*definitely* not nighttime winter outerwear, she thought. She pushed open the stable door and carefully closed it behind her. Horses snorted in their stalls. The place was lit with safety lights. Nancy moved away from the drafty door, into the tack room, and breathed in the musty smell of leather as she punched her dad's number on her cell phone. He picked up on the second ring.

"Dad, it's Nancy."

"Having a good time?" he asked.

"You could say that—but it's not exactly what I expected," she replied.

"Is there a problem? Is everyone okay?" His voice was filled with concern.

"Not to worry, Dad, nothing I can't handle." Then she filled him in on the situation at the resort. She told him about how Lauren had arranged for a food critic to visit the resort, and how Nancy wondered exactly what her intentions were: to help Mike and Jillian, or to hurt them? Nancy asked her father about Lauren and Mike's relationship.

Carson cleared his throat before speaking. "Originally their breakup was pretty nasty. Mainly because of the business. Lauren had wanted to open a resort, exactly like Gourmet Getaway. They didn't have the money, but they fought over the idea. Mike won out in the end by paying her a large settlement. Then Lauren got her television show and a whole new career in the gourmet cooking world, and now she seems pretty happy."

"Do you think she'd benefit from Mike's business failing?" Nancy inquired.

"I don't see how, financially. But there are always emotional issues between exes. Maybe Lauren is jealous of Jillian, or of Mike for realizing their old dream with a new wife." This was just what Nancy had suspected.

Next she asked him about Nate's rights to his cabin. Carson said he'd have to look into Massachusetts law to be sure, but if the actual deed to the property granted lifelong rights to Nate, they would continue no matter how many times the place changed hands. Nancy said good-bye, hung up, then put the phone in her pocket.

As she passed through the tack room door something whizzed by her head. She heard a dull clunking sound and a horse's whinny. Then, all at once, the lights went out, the stable door slammed, and a latch clanked into its cradle.

8

Food Fright

The thunk of the latch was followed by the sound of footsteps receding quickly from the front of the stable. Without stopping to feel for the light switch, Nancy hurled herself in the direction of the door. She tripped over something and stumbled into a pile of straw on the stable floor. She fell hard on her side and heard a ripping sound as she went down.

"My dress!" She groaned. She ran her hand down the length of her skirt until her fingers touched something cold and curved, with a pointed end. It was a hook of some sort, nailed low on the wall outside the tack room.

Nancy took a minute to gather her wits about her, then felt in her jacket pocket. Her fingers closed around her trusty penlight. She pulled it out, turned it on, and examined her immediate surroundings. First she unsnagged her dress from the hook, got up, and rubbed the side of her hip where she'd fallen. She'd be black and blue later, but she was okay. Then she aimed the light back toward the tack room. *Something* had whizzed by her head—but what?

Light from her flashlight glinted off something embedded in one of the thick wooden support posts just inside the tack room. As Nancy drew closer, the blood drained from her face. Half-buried in the thick four-by-four was the blade of a short-handled ax. Someone had thrown it at her before turning off the lights.

Nancy realized her hands were shaking. This went far beyond messages inscribed in red paint. If someone had just wanted to scare her, they had certainly succeeded. She swallowed hard, then steadied her nerves. Mike was going to have to call the police now.

With her flashlight aimed toward the stable door, Nancy spotted the light switch. She turned the light on and tried to open the door, but found that it was latched from the outside. She shouted a couple of times for someone to open the door, then gave up. Dinner would be served soon; most staff and guests were probably in the main building. The chances of a passerby hearing her were slim.

Nancy could see fading twilight through the narrow chink between the door and the door frame.

With the right tool she could lift the latch, but she didn't have anything on her except the penlight.

She went back into the tack room and looked around. On one wall hooks held assorted bits, bridles, and reins. Saddles were stored on saddle racks against another wall. Above the saddles was a pegboard with shelving. Nancy spotted a red metal toolbox on one shelf. She couldn't reach it, so she piled up two bales of hay, climbed on them, and took down the box. It didn't take long to spot what she needed: a stiff but slim metal file.

Before she went back to the door, she stopped and stared at the ax. Nancy was tempted to leave it where it was, then realized whoever threw the ax might come back to retrieve it. Taking off her jacket, she wrapped the sleeve around the ax handle and yanked the ax out of the beam. Then she tucked it in a dark corner behind the rack of saddles. To be sure no one could find it, she propped a bale of hay in front of the saddle rack. The police would have to check out the prints, but Nancy was pretty sure she knew whose ax it was.

Nancy went back to the door, and after a couple of attempts she managed to jiggle the latch upward with the file. She pushed open the big door, burst into the barnyard, and slammed right into Monica's chest.

"Hey!" Monica exclaimed. She was still dressed in

jodhpurs, a thick cream woolen turtleneck, and an expensive riding jacket, and she was on her cell phone and holding a bridle in the other hand. "Watch where you're going!" she said, quickly adjusting the scarf on her head and looking extremely upset. Monica gave Nancy a critical look.

"Whatever happened to you?" she asked, her eyes traveling from Nancy's face to her jacket, and then to the skirt of her dress. She frowned. "Not you—someone else," she said to whomever was on the phone. "Gotta go." When she snapped her cell phone shut, it emitted a familiar electronic tune.

"Why are you lurking out here?" she asked Nancy, tucking her cell phone in the pocket of her riding jacket. "And dressed like *that*?"

"Lurking?" Nancy repeated in disbelief. She swallowed her anger and tried to control her voice. "Someone just locked me in that stable!"

Monica's expression instantly shifted. "What?" Her concern sounded genuine. "Why?"

"Good question," Nancy answered. "Did you see anyone out here? It was just a few minutes ago."

Monica shook her head. "No one." She hurried to add, "But I just got here. I was halfway up to my room to change when I remembered I left this bridle in the corral. So I came back to put it away."

"So you didn't see anyone?" Nancy asked again. Monica's story was plausible, but she seemed nervous or worried about something—and Nancy was pretty sure it had nothing to do with misplaced bridles.

"Nope. Not a soul. Now let me put this away. I'm freezing out here. And you better change before dinner."

"Right," Nancy said. She'd barely started across the barnyard when she looked back toward the stable. The light in the tack room was still on. Suddenly she realized why Monica's phone sounded familiar—it played the same tune as the one she'd overheard on the back porch the night before when the woman hung up.

Was Monica behind the vandalism? The woman had seemed a bit of a powder puff at first, but actually was rather athletic. Could she have thrown that ax? Possibly, but not probably. It had been thrown with considerable force by someone who was used to the weight of an ax.

Besides, what motive did Monica have for seeing the Getaway fail? Why did running into Nancy just now make her so jumpy?

At the moment Nancy had no idea, but she was determined to find out. Something about Monica didn't ring true.

"I thought you were wearing your blue dress," Hannah remarked a little later when Nancy came into the lounge. A buffet of hot hors d'oeuvres had been set up, and Nancy had filled her plate with a selection of the savory goodies before making her way over to her friends. Dressed in slim black pants and a peach sweater set, Bess sat demurely on the sofa next to Hannah and picked delicately at a miniature quiche. George, on the other hand, was sitting cross-legged on the floor, wearing a slitted jean skirt, black tights, and a red sweater.

Nancy laughed. "It was too cold for the dress," she said. Which certainly was the truth, or at least part of it. After returning from the stable, she'd hurried up the back stairs, relieved to find that Hannah had already gone down for dinner. She'd changed into brown tailored pants and a warm rust sweater that brought out the red in her hair. She'd have Hannah help her mend her dress later, but at the moment Nancy didn't want to alarm her.

"So can you guess which of these we made?" Bess asked as Nancy bit into an interesting-looking pastry with walnuts and cheese.

Nancy shook her head. "They all smell so delicious. What kind of cheese is this?"

"Goat cheese," Hannah told her. "I worked on those, and Bess made the little spinach pies. Fortunately there were no more disasters in the kitchen." She got up from the sofa and waved at an older couple who were having drinks in a corner. "I'm going to join my new friends over there. Turns out the man knows a cousin of mine who lives in Baltimore!"

Nancy waited until Hannah had left, then, lowering her voice, she told Bess and George about the incident with the ax.

"Nancy!" Bess cried in horror.

George put her hand over Bess's mouth. "Not so loud," she admonished.

Bess pushed away her cousin's hand and continued in a soft, frightened voice. "You could have been killed. You *have* to call the police, or at least talk to Mike."

"I talked to him this afternoon in the stable, but that was before I got trapped," Nancy admitted.

"You had this conversation in the stable?" George asked. "Nancy, what if someone else was there and overheard you?"

Nancy thought back. "There *was* a noise back in the stalls. I thought it was a horse, but maybe someone was there. The person probably heard that I was trying to track down the source of the vandalism—"

"And they wanted to scare you off. It wouldn't be the first time someone tried to force you off a case," George reminded her.

"Do you think Nate's behind this?" Bess asked. "He's got an ax."

Nancy shook her head. "We don't know that he's the only one around here with an ax, Bess. I never got a close look at his ax. This one could have been his, or maybe not. Lots of people have axes in the country, particularly on a farm with a wood lot."

"Do you think there are any other suspects?"

Nancy looked at George. "Maybe, but nothing seems to connect. The only obvious possibility is Nate, but Mike is sure that sabotage isn't Nate's style." Nancy was tempted to share her suspicions of Monica and Lauren, and that mysterious cell phone conversation. She was too unsure of what their motives would be, though, and whom either one might be working with. While Monica *might* have thrown that ax, Lauren definitely looked as though she didn't have an athletic bone in her small body.

As they took their places in the dining room a little while later, Monica entered the room. She smiled coolly at Nancy before sitting down. "Different outfit," she said, arching her eyebrows.

"Warmer than a dress," Nancy said, noticing that Monica was wearing a cashmere sheath that clung to her figure.

Monica nodded, then turned back to her brother and sister-in-law. Nancy tried to keep one ear trained on their conversation, but Bess was pulling her sleeve.

"Doesn't dinner smell great?" she said.

"Cadot has worked his usual miracles," Oscar

Sanchez spoke up from the next table. Nancy turned her chair so the two parties could talk more easily with each other.

"Don't forget, it wasn't the chef who supervised in the kitchen tonight," Bess reminded him. "It was Lauren."

"But Lauren followed Cadot's recipe to a tee. I can't wait to eat the stuffing." Hannah then went on to list the ingredients. To Nancy's ears the combination of walnuts and truffles sounded like pure music.

"But that's not all—he does something unique with cabbage, figs, and apricots," Hannah continued.

"Sounds interesting," Monica commented.

George laughed. "Hey, aren't you the one who's not into all this gourmet stuff?"

Isabelle Sanchez exchanged a quick glance with Monica before speaking. "Trust me, she's not. I was filling her in on the usual sorts of things a chef might put inside a pheasant."

Before Monica could say anything else, Naomi and another server, an older guy with glasses, walked up. Each server was carrying a heavy tray. With one hand the man opened up a collapsible serving table and helped Naomi set her tray next to his on the surface. Each tray held a large covered platter.

Naomi took the cover off the first platter. Two well-browned and roasted pheasants were nestled in a bed of ruffled, red-leafed lettuce. The whole platter was garnished with fresh figs, dried apricots, and sprigs of green herbs.

"Beautiful!" Hannah exclaimed.

"Looks almost too good to eat," Nancy remarked.

"Not to me!" George said. "I'm starving."

Naomi set the platter on the table, picked up a carving knife and a long-handled fork, and carefully began cutting the pheasant into two halves. Nancy glanced up at the vegetarian's face. Her nose was wrinkled in obvious distaste, but she wielded the knife with considerable skill. The bird was so tender that the knife seemed to slide through it as if it were butter. The pheasant fell open and the fragrance of the stuffing wafted up. Nancy's mouth began to water.

"Oh, this is incredible," Bess exclaimed as Naomi set a plate with half a pheasant in front of her. She spooned some sauce over the bird and stuffing. After she finished serving Nancy's table, Naomi turned to the Sanchez party.

Again she removed the cover from the platter, picked up the carving knife, and began cutting through the first bird. Suddenly she let out a low grunt, and Nancy looked up from her supper. Naomi was struggling with the knife. It didn't seem to want to slice through the bird. She had struggled only a minute when Mike walked up behind her.

"Problem?" he asked, flashing a nervous smile at the Sanchezes.

"Maybe something happened to the knife," Naomi mumbled, looking flustered.

Mike took the knife from her and had her step aside. "The knife looks fine. Maybe you've got the wrong angle."

He began to frown. "What's going on here?" His knuckles whitened as he forced the knife through whatever was resisting the blade. Using the fork, he pried the pheasant open. A smoky chemical odor rose out of the cavity. As the stuffing spilled out, Mike gasped in horror and dropped the knife.

Embedded in the stuffing was a half-melted rubber glove.

9

Cooking Up a Storm

Horrified, Monica jumped up and tossed her napkin on the floor. "This is beyond disgusting!"

Every eye in the room turned toward her table. "It's repulsive," she continued. Nancy craned her neck. "Repulsive" sure described the awful smell, and the sight of the melted fingers of the glove oozing into the stuffing was enough to turn anyone's stomach.

"Mr. Rinaldi, be forewarned: Before I leave town, I'm reporting you people to the health department," Monica threatened.

Nancy caught her breath. That was all Mike needed.

Mike turned ashen. "Ms. Sanchez, please. Cadot wasn't in the kitchen to oversee things. Someone was careless. I'll bring you whatever you want for dinner—we have other specialties tonight, and—"

Monica waved him off with her hand. "Forget it. I've got a granola bar in my room. That'll tide me over until I leave tomorrow morning. I don't trust anything from your kitchen."

"Monica, please, calm down." Isabelle got up. She put her hand on Monica's shoulder. "This was an accident."

"This place has too many 'accidents,'" Monica insisted as Lauren came out of the kitchen. "What's clear," Monica fumed, "is that this resort is plagued by sloppy management! If you and Oscar want to stay, that's your business. I can find my own way home."

"Ms. Sanchez?" Lauren said. "Please, if there's a problem, let us try to help."

"'Us'?" a soft voice repeated tightly from right behind Nancy. She looked up to see Jillian. She must have come in from the front desk. How long had she been standing there? Jillian shot an angry glance at Lauren, then visibly struggled to master herself. Clearing her throat, she clapped her hands together and addressed the room. "Sorry, there's been a problem here. Please continue to enjoy your dinners." Dropping her voice she said to Mike, "Get rid of that thing *now*. I'll deal with the guests."

Turning to Monica, she put out both her hands in a pleading gesture. "Monica, if there is anything I can do to make up for this . . ."

Monica gave an annoyed snort and marched off without answering. Lauren hurried after her.

"Oscar, Isabelle, what can we do for you?" Jillian positioned herself between them and the serving table while Mike and Naomi picked up both trays. As they headed for the kitchen, Nancy followed, not waiting to hear the Sanchezes respond to Jillian.

The kitchen door had barely swung shut when Naomi tore off her apron. The two sous-chefs Lauren had called in earlier looked up from the stove. Cadot's young helpers were whispering to each other. When Mike walked in, they traded nervous looks, then went back to silently filling customer orders. Nancy realized news of the latest dining disaster had already reached the kitchen.

Mike took the platter off the tray and put it on the counter. "Deal with this," he told Naomi.

The girl averted her eyes from the ruined pheasant. "I—I can't!" she stammered. She didn't just look revolted and a little green, she looked plain frightened. *Why would she be scared?* Nancy wondered. Without another word Naomi bolted out of the kitchen. Nancy heard the door to the staff lounge slam.

Nancy turned to see that Mike was about to dump the pheasant, glove, and stuffing into the garbage.

"Stop!" she cried, blocking his way. "Let me look at this first."

Mike froze. "Why?"

Nancy glanced around the kitchen. Everyone was riveted to his or her job, but Nancy knew people were listening. She lowered her voice. "Evidence, Mike."

He put the tray down and let Nancy examine the steamy mess. "I was hoping this really was an accident. Ever the optimist," he added ruefully.

Nancy's suspicions were instantly confirmed. Grabbing a fork, she gingerly lifted one of the fingers of the rubber glove. It wasn't one of those thin latex gloves used by kitchen workers. It was heavier yellow rubber—the same sort Hannah used when washing dishes. It had been propped inside the cavity of the pheasant with toothpicks. She stepped aside for Mike to see. "Now there's no question that someone's determined to make your restaurant look bad."

"But who? Who would do this?"

Who would have had a chance to? Nancy thought. *Who had access to the kitchen?* She'd query George later to see if someone outside of the usual staff had been hanging out during dinner preparations. But at the moment the first possibility that came to mind was Lauren. "Mike, I hate to suggest this," she said gently, "but we can't rule anyone out at this point. Lauren was in charge of things here just now."

"Lauren?" Mike repeated in a shocked whisper. "Why would *she* do this? She's rooting for this place. She's arranged for the food critic to come. She's even making a video to promote us."

100

Publicity can work to promote, or *to demolish,* Nancy thought. The video footage Lauren's crew had shot—first of the incident in town, and then of the chef's outbursts earlier in the kitchen—painted an unflattering picture of the resort.

To Mike, though, she admitted, "It's just a possibility. I think there are other suspects too." She told him about the ax incident and about her suspicions of Nate.

"You think Nate did that?" Mike looked doubtful. "What about this glove thing . . . how could he do that?"

"I haven't a clue. And I have no idea how he missed me, if he threw the ax. He's a pretty experienced woodsman and hunter." Nancy sighed, then looked at the platter. The pheasant was lukewarm but still smelled awful. "We can toss this now," she said, sweeping the food into the garbage herself.

By the time dinner was over, the weather outside the Getaway had changed. The wind had shifted and was blowing warm air from the south. The clear cold afternoon had given way to a miserable, wet night. But a little rain couldn't keep Nancy from going to town for that conflict resolution meeting between the animal rights groups and the local hunters.

After the three girls changed into jeans, Bess and George went down to on the front porch, and Nancy went for the car. At the last minute Mike had cancelled the dessert cooking class, and Bess had decided to come along to the meeting. "Ryan might be there," she had told Nancy. "He's into animal rights."

As Nancy went for the car, she thought about Ryan. She hadn't seen him since running into him in the yard earlier that afternoon. Bess was right. He probably took the night off to go to the meeting.

By the time she reached the parking area, the light rain had turned into a heavy downpour. Once inside the van, Nancy wiped the rain off her face and turned on the ignition. When she backed out of the parking place, her headlights arced across the rain-swept barnyard. They illuminated someone standing beneath the narrow overhang of the chicken house with his or her back turned. The person was gesturing vehemently to a second person, who was shrouded in shadow. As Nancy's lights swept the area, the first figure looked up. It was a woman, and she was holding something in her hand. She quickly stuffed it into her pocket, but not before Nancy saw it was a rubber glove—the same sort that had been inside the pheasant.

Startled by the light, the woman ducked into the shadows. The hood of her poncho was up, but before she turned, Nancy caught a good look at her face. It was Naomi.

A bunch of questions flooded Nancy's thoughts. What was she doing with that glove anyway? Was it the same one Nancy had thrown in the garbage earlier—or was it the mate to it? Could Naomi be behind the sabotage? And why would she want to see the inn fail? Was being a vegetarian enough of a motive? And who was with her just now? A coconspirator? Naomi had seemed genuinely freaked out when she saw that glove in the pheasant, Nancy remembered as she drove up to the Getaway's front porch. Almost as freaked out as when she saw the painted words on Cadot's door. Either she was innocent or a really good actress.

By the time Nancy arrived at the Waringham town hall, almost all the parking spots had been taken. George looked at the rain streaming down the windshield and remarked, "I can't believe how many people have turned up for a town meeting on a night like this."

"I can't believe *I* turned up!" Bess grumbled. "My hair is going to be a wreck—and what if Ryan really is here?"

"I doubt he'll be interested in your hair," Nancy said as they made a beeline for the white clapboard building. "He's probably going to have his mind on the meeting, not on chatting up girls."

Inside, the place smelled of wet wool and too many bodies crowded in a small, overheated space. People milling around the refreshment table created a bottleneck just inside the door. Nancy, Bess, and George squeezed past, too full from dinner to want coffee and donuts.

Rows of metal folding chairs filled the square hall. Up front a low platform ran the width of the room. A woman stood at the podium, holding a gavel and talking to Matt, the storekeeper, and another man who had long dreadlocks and a gentle face. Nancy pegged the latter man as the spokesman for the animal rights contingent.

When most of the crowd was finally seated, the meeting was called to order. The woman, who introduced herself as Maddy Alson, Waringham's selectwoman, introduced the people on the podium: Matt Greely, who ran the general store, and Jon Bovier, the president of the local chapter of a national animal rights organization.

A loud and heated debate began immediately after the introductions. It seemed Jon and Matt were the only voices of moderation.

Hunters were scornful of the animal rights activists, and hurled accusations of them being dreamy tree-huggers who had no understanding of how conservation really worked.

Animal rights extremists chanted the word "murderers" every time a prohunting speaker took the floor.

Suddenly George prodded Nancy. "Look who's here!" Nancy turned just as Nate Caldwell leaped to his feet.

"What's wrong with this picture?" he bellowed,

gesturing broadly around the room. His eyes lit on Nancy. "City folk. That's what," he said, briefly singling her out with a glance. "Yeah—city folk who don't respect rural ways. These city folk turn up with new-fangled ideas, run people out of town whose great great grandfolks built this community. They think killing deer means we hate nature. We love nature. We're part of it—and unlike these people, we haven't forgotten it."

He pumped his hand in the air. Half the room cheered, half booed. He basked in the attention, then added in a more serious tone, "Hunters these days are the only predators left to help check the deer population. Hunting organizations are responsible for bringing back all sorts of wildlife to this area. I bet our forests are richer in game now than they were two hundred years ago." Another cheer went up, and he plunked himself down in his seat.

"Didn't think he had that in him," George remarked.

Neither did Nancy. Nate was a surprisingly strong speaker. He made sense, too—though she felt she didn't know enough about the issue to agree with him. But he clearly had a point. Nancy was sure people like Ryan and Naomi didn't understand Nate's traditions, and his own version of love for the land.

No sooner had Nancy thought about Naomi than she walked in. Her hair was soaking wet, and her poncho was streaming water. The only empty seats were up front by the platform. Shyly Naomi sidled down the aisle. As she passed Nancy she gave her a nervous smile.

Nancy smiled back, but wondered why the girl was being so friendly. Maybe she hadn't recognized Nancy's van back in the barnyard.

When the moderator called a break, Bess and George went to get coffee. Nancy, however, went straight up to Naomi. She didn't mince words. "I saw you earlier outside the chicken house at the Getaway. I was in the parking lot. Who were you with?"

Naomi's eyes widened and her cheeks reddened. "No one. I mean, I wasn't anywhere near the chicken house tonight. I left the Getaway a little after that disgusting scene." She paused, then added, "I felt a little sick, so I went home before I came here."

Nancy refused to back down. The girl was out-and-out lying—and she wanted to know why. "I don't know what you've got to hide, Naomi, but I saw you. And you were holding a glove—just like the one we found stuffed in the pheasant."

"You've got to be kidding," Naomi defended herself. "Whatever you think you saw, it wasn't me. I don't know anything about any glove."

Before Nancy could press her point further, Naomi turned on her heels and walked away.

As Nancy returned to her seat, she saw Ryan had finally showed up. He was leaning against the wall just opposite her, talking to some of the animal rights activists.

Bess heaved a sigh. "I knew he'd be here. How's my hair look?"

Nancy turned and regarded Bess's hair. The heat inside the room had dried it, and it had fluffed up around her face. "It actually looks great, Bess."

George gave Bess a friendly poke and whispered, "Don't look now, but I get the impression Ryan thinks so too."

Nancy turned slowly. Sure enough, Ryan was looking right at them. He caught Nancy's eye and winked. Nancy hazarded a smile, but her eyes were fixed on Ryan's feet. "Ryan dressed for the occasion," she said.

George looked past Bess and Nancy and gave a low whistle of appreciation. "New boots. Guess his old ones wore out," she added.

Nancy frowned. "Does he usually wear boots?"

"Yeah. I guess he's on his feet so much, in the kitchen and the yard. They're better than sneakers," George explained.

Matt took the microphone and addressed the crowd. "I see that one of our more active animal rights advocates has finally turned up. Ryan, you're a newcomer to the community, but already everyone knows you." A ripple of applause and a chorus of low groans greeted Matt's words. He waited for the audience to quiet down before addressing Ryan again. "How do you suggest we come to a compromise here, or at least open better channels of communication than violent protest and vandalism?"

Ryan lifted his shoulders. "I actually came to learn and listen. I've heard about these mediation meetings. I wanted to see how—and if—they work."

Nancy noticed that several of the animal rights people looked disappointed. Then someone else took the floor, and the arguments continued. In a short time the meeting was adjourned. Folks milled around, talking, while some people helped fold up the chairs. Nancy carried her chair up to the front of the room where a man was putting them into the closet. Naomi was nearby, struggling into her poncho. Before Nancy reached her, Ryan walked up. He bent over and whispered in her ear.

The color washed right out of Naomi's cheeks. She shook her head violently, then elbowed her way through the crowd and out the door. Ryan marched out after her. They looked like a couple in a fight.

"Since when are Ryan and Naomi an item?" Bess looked dismayed as she handed her chair to the people on the platform.

Nancy wasn't sure, but she had a strong hunch that it was Ryan with whom Naomi had been arguing a little while ago outside the chicken house. She was about to answer Bess when a huge explosion shook the room.

10

A Cruel Blow

The meeting hall instantly erupted in a string of screams and shouts.

"A bomb!" one voice shrieked as the crowd mobbed the exit.

"No, it's the boiler!" someone else yelled. Nancy stayed by the window. If there was a fire, she could get out that way. She didn't want to get crushed in the crowd. "George, Bess, don't panic!" she called out. She couldn't see them in the throng pushing toward the door.

"Call 911!" someone ordered.

"How? Cell phones don't work here!" Maddy could be heard above the general din. "I'll call from the booth outside if—"

She was cut off by another round of explosions.

Nancy's eye caught flashes of light coming from the parking lot. "It's not an explosion," she hollered. "Maddy! It's fireworks."

Maddy elbowed her way to a window and looked for herself. Then she hurried to the platform, grabbed the gavel, and pounded it on the podium. "Everyone, calm down. It's just fireworks." She cast Nancy a grateful look. "Good thing you happened to be by the window. I'm glad *someone* here stayed calm."

Nancy didn't feel calm. Her adrenaline was racing. The explosion had scared her too—and she realized that the series of weird events since she arrived at the Getaway were beginning to unnerve her. Nancy hated feeling scared, and now she was mad. "Whoever set them off was trying to break up this meeting," she said angrily to Maddy.

"It figures," Maddy said. She nodded at Nancy, then pounded her gavel. "Everyone, please come back in," she commanded.

Gradually the room quieted down. A few people filed back in. They clustered near the door. Ryan was there, and so was Nate. Naomi, however, was nowhere to be seen.

Maddy singled out Nate and Ryan. "Where were you two when the explosion happened just now?"

"Outside," Ryan admitted.

"Outside," Nate snapped.

"And you saw nothing?" Maddy suggested.

110

Nate shrugged. "Not a thing. Not that I was really paying attention. I was checking the sky. Rain's clearing out. Short-lived, that storm. Good hunting tomorrow." He half spat out the last words and looked directly at Ryan.

Ryan turned his back on Nate. "I was heading for my truck. It's across the street. I didn't see anything, or anyone. But the noise was pretty loud. Scary. Sounded like a bomb or gun. Something bad."

Maddy glared at both men, then she told everyone to leave.

On Maddy's way out, she thanked Nancy again. Nancy brushed it off, but said, "Too bad extremists are trying to derail your efforts to resolve things here."

Nate was right behind her. "Oh, listen to the little lady!"

Nancy turned. She and Nate traded glares.

Nate held Nancy's stare. "Seems to me whoever set that off had pretty good timing. Don't know who it was, but the hot air was getting a little thick to breathe in there."

Later that night when Nancy put herself to bed, Nate's words were still running through her head.

The next morning when the sky was still dark, George dragged Nancy out of bed to go for a run. Nancy tried to escape until George told her Monica would be joining them. Apparently Lauren had convinced her to stay for at least one more day.

Careful not to wake Hannah, Nancy dressed in the dark. She topped off a couple of layers of light sweaters with a hooded sweatshirt. Nancy went downstairs determined to use the run to find out more about Monica. She couldn't shake the feeling that the woman was hiding something. Monica just *had* to be lying about not seeing anyone around the stables after the ax incident the day before.

After an hour all Nancy had learned was that Monica was an awesome runner. Not even the steep, hilly terrain seemed to faze her. Maintaining a brisk pace, they ran all the way down to Waringham, then back. By the time they looped back to the barnyard, Nancy was winded and her legs were cramping.

She and George slowed to a walk as they neared the kitchen, but Monica split off. "I'm training for a marathon. I need to put in five more miles this morning," she said, jogging in place. With a quick wave, and still looking fresh, she disappeared down the misty trail.

At the chicken house Nancy bent over to catch her breath. "That woman is amazing."

George put her leg on the railing of a fence and stretched out her muscles. "Sometimes she's totally bad news. Today she was sort of fun."

"I wouldn't go *that* far," Nancy said, working the

112

knots out of her calves. "More like *neutral,* as opposed to *obnoxious.*"

"Touché." George chuckled.

They finished stretching, then sauntered toward the main building. The sun was still behind the hills, but the sky was pink and swirls of mist rose from the kitchen garden. Nancy glanced at Cadot's cottage. His window was still dark, just like all the windows in the inn—except for a square of yellow light that filled the kitchen window. The window was open slightly, and the sound of voices drifted out into the yard.

"Hey, someone's up!" George said.

"Better yet"—Nancy grinned—"someone's cooking. I smell something wonderful baking."

As they drew near, Nancy's smile quickly faded. "Sounds like someone's arguing," she whispered. "Given what's been going on around here, I'm guessing that whoever is fighting isn't arguing about the best recipe for muffins."

Stealthily both girls approached the window. Nancy tried to peer in, but the pane was steamed up from the heat inside the kitchen. She managed to make out two figures at the kitchen counter. "I think that's Mike," she whispered. "He's arguing with someone."

George looked over Nancy's shoulder. "Hey, there are three people, and—"

George's next words were cut off by a grunt and a sickening thud.

113

Nancy turned around to see George crumpled, unconscious, on the porch. "George!" she gasped. Then she saw someone in a ski mask. He or she—Nancy couldn't tell which—was pressed against the side of the building, out of sight of the window, with a frying pan in one gloved hand. As Nancy watched in horror, the figure lifted the pan, and aimed the base right at her.

Nancy swerved and darted out of the way. Her assailant lost his or her balance for a moment. Nancy seized the opportunity to attack. Spinning around, she used her momentum to aim a karate kick at the assailant's midsection—but Nancy's own balance was skewed, and she missed. She instantly regained her footing and charged the masked person again. Nancy threw up her arm, deflecting her attacker's hand. But the assailant was as agile as Nancy—and also apparently trained in martial arts. As Nancy aimed another blow on her attacker, a foot came out and tripped her. Before she fell, she felt the bottom of the pan slam against her skull.

"George!" she cried before a searing pain enveloped her, and she plummeted into total darkness.

11

A Secret Revealed

"Nancy! Nancy!" The sound of her name drifted slowly into Nancy's consciousness. Part of her knew she should answer. It was time to open her eyes.

"Nancy, please. Say something."

The voice was familiar, but Nancy couldn't place it. Then a hand touched the crown of her head, setting off ripples of excruciating pain. "Ow!" she cried out.

"You're okay. You're okay!" That was George's voice. As the pain subsided Nancy remembered everything. The figure with the mask. The frying pan. She forced her eyes open, and slowly the face peering down at her came into focus. It wasn't George. It was Monica. She was still in her running clothes. She'd peeled off her gloves and was patting Nancy's hand. What was she doing here?

"George," Nancy managed to say. "Where is she?"

"Over here." George sounded a bit weak. "Guess my head's harder than yours. I came to just as Monica jogged up. She propped me against the wall here and then helped you."

Nancy struggled to sit up. She forced back a wave of nausea and refused to give in to the dizziness. Monica put her hand against Nancy's back. "Don't move too fast." Then Monica began pounding on the kitchen window. "Hey, someone!" she called through the window. "I need help! Nancy and George are hurt."

Leaning on Monica's arm, Nancy gradually got up, steadying herself against the building.

Mike appeared at the kitchen door and cried in alarm at the sight of Nancy and George. "What happened?"

"Someone hit them both on the head!" Monica said.

She and Mike helped Nancy into the kitchen. George followed slowly on her own. Once inside, Monica eased Nancy into a chair, then glared at Mike as he got both girls some water. "What is going on around here anyway?" She sounded like she was blaming Mike personally. "This was no accident." Monica stopped and looked outside the kitchen window onto the porch. "Someone attacked both these girls. It's bad enough you're plagued with unexplainable kitchen disasters, but this is criminal. I hope you intend to do something about it."

While Monica ranted, the pain in Nancy's head

subsided to a dull ache. A couple of aspirin and she'd be all right. Then Nancy remembered Mike had been in the kitchen just before she and George had been attacked. Someone had been with him. Two people, actually—Nancy recalled George saying something about that. But now there was only Mike, Nancy, George, and Monica.

"What were you girls doing out there?" Mike asked. "Did you see who attacked you?"

Before Nancy could answer, Jillian came in. She was wearing a ski hat and mittens. "Hi, guys," she said, but the minute she saw Nancy she gasped. "What happened to you?" She hurried over to Nancy. "Mike, call a doctor."

"I don't need a doctor," Nancy assured her as the door leading to the pantry and kitchen office flew open. "What's this about doctors?" Lauren stood there wearing her coat. At the sight of Nancy she rushed over and put a hand on her forehead. Lauren's fingers were like ice.

"They were outside on the porch and someone attacked them," Monica declared.

"Why in the world were you out so early?" Lauren asked the girls.

"We'd been jogging," Nancy said quickly, before George could let anything slip about how they heard an argument. "We were hungry, and when we saw the light we thought we'd get some breakfast."

"You both look like you can use ice packs," Jillian said, heading for the freezer.

"And coffee," Mike added.

"Coffee would be good," George said, then eyed the muffin tin on the counter. "And maybe a muffin."

"I'll just take an ice pack." Nancy gingerly touched her head. "My stomach feels a bit shaky. I'll eat after my shower."

Lauren gave George a muffin, then left.

"Well, if you girls are okay, I'm going upstairs to shower and change," Monica said. She wiped her brow and left the room.

Nancy followed a little while later. She climbed the back stairs slowly, then made her way down the hall. She felt sore all over, though the blow had been only to her head. Probably from the running, she figured. When she rounded the corner she saw that Monica's door, at the end of the corridor, was ajar.

Good, she thought. She was eager to talk to Monica. The woman had to have seen someone in the yard after Nancy and George were attacked. Unless . . .

A terrible thought slowly formed in Nancy's mind: unless the assailant had been Monica herself. If only she could remember what the person had been wearing. But the blow to her head had addled her brain. She remembered the ski mask and frying pan, but no other details.

Suddenly someone came out of Monica's room. It

was Lauren, not Monica. As Nancy watched, Lauren tucked a sheaf of papers under her coat. Instinctively Nancy ducked into an empty room and waited behind the door until she heard Lauren's footsteps pass.

Cautiously Nancy poked her head out into the hall. It was empty. But what had Lauren been doing in Monica's room? Although Nancy was tempted to follow Lauren, her gut told her to confront Monica. Could it really be a coincidence that Monica just happened to turn up immediately after both times Nancy was attacked? Nancy didn't think so.

Monica's door was still cracked open. Nancy knocked, then walked in. The lights were on and the shower was running in the bathroom, but the room was empty.

Nancy was about to leave when she noticed a laptop on a small writing desk. It was open and the screen saver—a slide show of exotic chocolate desserts—was active. This meant the computer was on. Nancy hesitated for a moment, then quietly moved to the desk and touched the mouse.

The screen instantly came to life. With disappointment Nancy saw it was empty. She ran her eye across the top of the screen and realized it was open to a word processing program—the same one she used back home on her own computer. But the page was blank.

Nancy glanced back over her shoulder. The

shower was still on, and she could now hear Monica singing in a surprisingly good voice. On a hunch, Nancy took the mouse, pointed it to the "undo" icon, and clicked.

Instantly a page of double-spaced text appeared. Just as Nancy was about to read it, she heard the shower go off. Monica was still singing.

Nancy hurried toward the door. On her way, something on the top of the bureau caught her eye. Perched at a cocky angle, on a Styrofoam mannequin head, was Monica's gloriously thick dark hair. A wig!

Before Nancy's brain could process that discovery, she suddenly realized the singing in the bathroom had stopped. She whirled around and faced the bathroom door just as it flew open.

"What are you doing here?"

Nancy stared at the stranger. She clutched a silk kimono and her short hair was wet. It was darker than it would be dry, but the woman was definitely blond.

"Where's Monica?" Nancy exclaimed. Then Nancy took a closer look at the woman. "Wait. *You're* Monica." She looked from the woman back to the wig. Nancy went to grab it, but Monica got to it first.

"Nancy, what exactly are you doing in my room?"

Nancy improvised quickly. "I came in to thank you for helping out there on the porch, and to ask if you'd seen anyone."

For a long moment, Monica stood defiantly—but

beneath the defiance, Nancy clearly saw the woman was defensive, frightened, and annoyed—big-time. "Oh, what's the use!" The challenge in her eyes suddenly vanished. Monica plopped down on the bed, still clutching her robe with one hand. Nancy's whole body tensed up. Was Monica about to burst into tears and confess to all the vandalism—even today's attack?

Instead Monica began to laugh. It was a whole-body laugh, completely at odds with the sophisticated, snide woman Monica had been a few minutes before.

Nancy's temper began to rise. "I don't see what's so funny."

Monica struggled to control herself. "I'm sorry," she said, wiping the tears of laughter from her cheeks. "But I guess the cat's out of the bag now. So why shouldn't I tell you the truth?" She heaved a sigh. "My name isn't Monica Sanchez. In fact, I'm not remotely related to Oscar and Isabelle. They're just two of my favorite dining partners. You see, I'm Sylvia Green. I write under the name M. L. Gray."

The name rang a vague bell with Nancy. "Who?"

"The food critic."

"*You're* the critic?" Nancy looked at the wig Monica—or Sylvia, if that was her real name—was holding. Of course. The critic would want to be incognito.

Sylvia continued, "I'm the regular restaurant reviewer for *Epicure's Delight*. When the food editor for the *Offbeat and Great Eats Travel Guide* called and asked me to write a feature on this place, I jumped at the chance. The Getaway's new, but its reputation is already outstanding." She gave an annoyed, very Monica-like toss of her head. "Though, *why* beats me!"

Nancy studied the woman carefully. She seemed in some ways so different, so much more natural— and certainly less obnoxious—than she'd been until now that Nancy felt compelled to believe her about her real identity. Still, part of Nancy was skeptical. "Look, Monica—or Sylvia, whatever I'm supposed to call you now—how do I know you're telling the truth? There have been so many minor and huge catastrophes at the Getaway these past few days—ever since you arrived, I might add. How do I know you're not behind them?"

"Me? You think *I* have something to do with all this disgusting weirdness?" Monica looked genuinely offended.

"For instance, you insisted you didn't see anyone come out of the stables yesterday. But that's impossible. If you're telling the truth and had just come back from the corral, that is. Someone had just locked me in from the outside." Nancy omitted the part about the ax.

"No way. Someone locked you in?" Again Monica's face registered pure surprise. Then she frowned. "I wasn't lying. When Jillian skipped the trail ride, I grabbed the chance to use my cell phone and talk to my editor while I was on the trail. I hit a dead zone, so I phoned him back when I got to the corral. I really didn't see anyone. Not that I was looking." She looked up at Nancy. "I was behind the chicken house, out of the wind, checking my notes. Anyone could have walked past and I wouldn't have seen them."

Monica's explanation made sense. "And about your disguise . . . ?" Nancy's eyes came to rest again on the hairpiece. Now that she realized it was a wig, the hair definitely looked too good to be true.

Monica groaned. "Awful, no? Imagine wearing that wig for days on end. Talk about a hassle! It was always slipping, and I was so afraid it would fall off whenever I went for a run or a ride." Monica stopped and took a hard look at Nancy. "But what's all this to you? You seem awfully involved for someone who's just a friend of Mike's."

Nancy wasn't ready to answer that. She was almost ready to rule out Monica as a suspect. Then again, Monica had some sort of connection to Lauren, and Lauren's actions—at least just now—seemed awfully suspicious. "Speaking of friends, I just remembered," Nancy said, sidestepping Monica's question, "Lauren's your friend, right?"

Monica's eyebrows shot up. "She told you that?"

"No. But she warned Mike that a critic was coming. She never said who."

"The little skunk!" Monica chuckled. "I'll deal with her later. She wasn't supposed to warn him. But what made you ask about Lauren?"

"I was wondering what she wanted just now. I saw her leave your room before I came in."

"Lauren? In here? Now?" Monica frowned, then shrugged. "I guess I was already in the shower and didn't hear her. I'll find out what she wanted later."

"You mean you didn't give her those papers?"

"What papers?" Monica asked.

"The ones she was carrying when I saw her in the hall," Nancy answered.

Monica jumped off the bed and hurried to the desk. A small printer was set up on the window seat behind the desk. She turned to Nancy, her face livid. "I don't believe this. The printout of my review is missing!"

12

Out of the Frying Pan . . .

"You think Lauren stole it?" Nancy asked. "Why would she do that?"

Monica let out an exasperated sigh. "Because I wouldn't let her read it. She's been bugging me all weekend about it. But I told her when I decided to take on the job that she had to stay out of it and keep her mouth shut. Some people," Monica muttered.

Suddenly her face brightened. "Oh, but it's still on the computer." She touched the mouse on her laptop and the screen saver gave way to a monitor full of text. "Thank goodness!"

"Actually," Nancy said, coming up behind Monica, "when you were in the shower, I touched the mouse. The screen was blank. Your article had been deleted— probably by Lauren. I took a chance and clicked the 'undo' icon, and, voilà, it reappeared. Apparently Lauren didn't think to delete it from your directory."

"Why in the world would she want to destroy my article?" Monica cried in dismay.

Nancy had a couple of theories, but all she said was, "Maybe she didn't want you to give the Getaway and Mike a bad review."

"A bad review?" Monica laughed a tight little laugh. "I guess, given what's been going on around here, she might very well think that." Looking back at Nancy, Monica made a face. "Actually I don't know *what* I think yet. This is just a draft. Here, read it." She stepped aside so Nancy could read the screen.

Nancy skimmed over the first couple of paragraphs. They dealt with the location and theme of the resort. Then Nancy read aloud: "'Considering the bizarre series of events that occurred during my stay here, the service was good, and the few uneventful meals were delicious. But a stay here might not be every guest's idea of a relaxing gourmet vacation.'" A couple of half-finished sentences were followed by a row of dots.

"That's where I got stuck," Monica explained when she saw that Nancy had reached the end of the article. "So I don't know what Lauren will make of what I wrote. Anyway, I must say the bizarre happenings around here make me wonder if someone isn't out to undermine Mike's business," Monica mused.

"Mike is wondering the same thing too," Nancy

126

said. "I should leave you to get dressed. Sorry for intruding the way I did."

"Not to worry. Actually, I'm relieved that at least *someone* knows I'm not a snobbish, hard-to-please, nasty creature with weird hair." Monica laughed, but quickly turned serious. "Please don't blow my cover. It's really important. The Sanchezes know, and of course Lauren knows who I am, but I won't be able to publish my article in good faith if either Cadot or Mike finds out."

"My lips are sealed," Nancy told her. "And don't worry. Lauren hasn't told either Mike or Jillian who you are. They haven't a clue." Nancy was halfway to the door when she turned around. "I'm sorry I suspected you of something. But could you let me know if you see anything suspicious? Mike's actually asked me to help him track the vandals down."

"I'll keep eyes and ears open," Monica promised. "And don't forget, I'm 'Monica' around here, not 'Sylvia.'"

Nancy left and poked her head into George and Bess's room. "How are you doing?" she asked George. George was sitting cross-legged on the bed, nursing a mug of hot chocolate. Bess was curled in an overstuffed chair, basking in a patch of sunlight that streamed through the lace curtains.

"I could get used to this," George quipped, gesturing with her head toward her chocolate. "When

Hannah came down to the kitchen to check out what the chef planned for breakfast, she heard what happened. Not only did she make me a stack of her famous pancakes, but she whipped up a whole pot of this. Have some!" George motioned toward the desk. A pot of hot chocolate stood beside a couple of mugs on a tray. "By the way, Hannah's looking for you. I told her you probably missed her on your way to shower—"

"But it looks like you haven't taken it yet," Bess observed. "You look a little pale, Nancy."

"I'm fine," Nancy assured her. She picked up a cup and poured some hot chocolate. "This will tide me over until breakfast. I'll find Hannah later. In the meantime, George, do you remember anything about who hit you?" she asked.

"We were just trying to figure that out," George answered.

Bess gave a little shiver. "Too bad you can't remember anything about what you saw," she said to George.

Nancy squeezed her eyes shut a moment and tried to visualize the moment she had turned and seen George crumple to the ground. Details gradually began to surface. "There was red. Wait—the person was wearing a red down vest," she exclaimed. "There was a sweater, too. I got a glimpse of it. I think it was a ski sweater—one of those Norwegian or Irish ones. It was heavy." Nancy suddenly was sure of that. She could recall the scratchy feeling of the sweater when she had parried her attacker's hand.

"Monica was wearing a red down vest," George said quietly.

"And Jillian was wearing a ski sweater this morning," Bess added. "I saw her when I went down to the kitchen."

"And Lauren's hands were cold as ice when she touched my head, afterward in the kitchen," Nancy remembered. "She must have come into the kitchen from outside."

"And she had a coat on," George pointed out.

"So any one of them could have been outside at the time. I mean, we know Monica was," Bess said.

"Right." Nancy bit her lip. She was sure now, though, that Monica had only turned up after the attack to help. Without divulging Monica's secret, she couldn't explain that Monica was no longer a suspect. "Let's not jump to conclusions," she said. "One or all of these women could be involved."

"Only Monica is athletic enough to have knocked us both out, though," George reminded her.

Nancy looked unconvinced. "You never know. Beneath all that glamour and softness, Jillian is probably very fit. She might even know some martial arts moves. Same goes for Lauren. And let's not forget Nate. . . ." *And,* Nancy added to herself, *Naomi and Ryan.*

Mike had mentioned previous incidents at the Getaway that had started over the summer. Maybe they were connected to this latest, more violent round of criminal behavior. Nancy had no way of knowing until she solved the case, but things had certainly escalated in sync with Cadot's stint at the Getaway. This made Nancy lean toward suspecting the animal rights people rather than Nate. Still, it was hard to imagine Naomi bopping anyone over the head. But if she was motivated to see the inn closed down, or had been swayed by an extremist like Ryan, she might be involved—and she might have a partner.

"So what do you think, Nancy?"

Nancy looked up at the sound of Bess's voice. "Sorry, I was running things through in my head. I think maybe we should split up. George, why don't you go with Monica on that advanced riding trail trip I saw posted on the bulletin board last night. Keep an eye on her, and on whomever else turns up. Maybe Nate will show his face along the trail and try to play another dirty trick."

"What about me?" Bess said, looking a bit anxious. "I don't ride very well, and I was hoping to take a cooking class. Cadot is supervising a lesson in cooking with wild mushrooms."

"Great—we'll both go to that. I want to stick around here. I haven't had a chance to scope out the kitchen much. Maybe our culprit has left some clues there."

The afternoon sun glinted against the tall shiny stockpots on the stove. Fragrant steam from the various simmering stocks wafted through the kitchen. A venison roast was already in the oven. But Nancy was too engrossed in Chef Cadot's lecture on the preparation of wild mushrooms to pay much attention to the savory smells.

"Zee preparation of zee mushrooms is most important," the chef said. He was sitting on a high chair with his bandaged hand propped on a pillow on his lap. Naomi and Ryan were assisting him. Lauren, Mike, and even Jillian had joined the small group of guests for the lesson. "Today we have here some new mushrooms zat Naomi has so kindly gathered from the local forest—they are fresh, and we will use them for one of the side dishes. They will beautifully complement our mélange of wild and cultivated root vegetables."

With a gesture from the chef Ryan carried a basket of mushrooms from the prep table. Nancy was pleased that she could recognize a few chicken-of-the-woods after her walk with Naomi the day before. The rest of the basket was filled with lovely round mushrooms. Some were a creamy white color, and others were brown.

At Monsieur Cadot's request, Naomi explained that the round mushrooms were all in the puffball family and were particularly delicious. "I didn't have time yesterday to show you where I usually find them. They're deeper in the woods, on the fringes of the meadow and near Greywater Creek—out by Nate Caldwell's cabin."

Naomi and Ryan spread the mushrooms out on a couple of white flour-sack towels. The chef picked them over. "Zees eeez a very important step," he told them. "Zee problem with zee wild mushrooms is zat zee people hurry too fast to cook and eat them. It eeez very important to make sure you have not picked accidently zee ones that will make you sick or kill you." He then sorted through the mushrooms himself. He showed everyone how to clean the mushrooms with a little brush, insisting that they never be washed with water—otherwise, they get soggy during cooking. Cadot distributed a few among the guests to cut up, then told Ryan to prepare the rest.

Ryan returned to the prep table. Nancy watched as he neatly sliced them and put them in a large colander.

Meanwhile, the chef put Hannah to work at the stove. "We will sauté zeez in small batches, so as not to bruise them. We want zee mushrooms to stay beautiful. Beauty is half zee pleasure of eating zees food," he said, throwing a dollop of butter into one of the large sauté pans.

Nancy was bringing her own small bowl of sliced mushrooms over to Hannah when Nate Caldwell burst through the kitchen door.

"Rinaldi, this is the last straw!" Caldwell slammed the door shut. He was holding a wood and metal contraption: some kind of animal trap.

"Nate, please. We're having a class here. Can we talk outside?" Mike went up to Nate and tried to steer him back out the door.

Nate dropped the trap on the floor and stood his ground. "I'm not going anywhere!" he fumed. "Maybe to the cops," Nate said, his eyes glittering. "And maybe to a court of law. I'll *sue* you and this place. Make you so broke you'll have to run clear out of the county with your tail between your legs!"

Bess caught Nancy's eye. Nancy nodded slightly. Nate had just given himself the perfect motive for sabotage.

Mike was visibly struggling to stay calm. "Okay, now stop threatening lawsuits and tell me what happened."

"What *happened*?" Nate bellowed. He kicked the trap, and it skittered over toward Hannah and the stove. "Someone wrecked this when he or she set whatever was trapped in it free. That animal's probably so wounded by now that it's off dying some terrible slow death or being preyed on by some other animal." He glanced around the room, and his eyes lit on Naomi. "Keep that in mind, girl, next time you try to free a rabbit!"

Naomi started to protest. "I never—"

Mike interrupted. "I doubt Naomi had anything to do with your traps. But I will talk to my staff. I'm thinking of getting some security out here for a while too, and they'll keep an eye on things."

"Security—ha!" Nate scoffed, stomping across the room to retrieve his equipment. He bent down and grabbed it. As he straightened up, he glanced at the stove. Ryan's colander full of mushrooms was off to the side. It was already half-empty, as Hannah was already cooking another batch in a second sauté pan.

"Mushrooms," Nate said. "Wild mushrooms."

"Yes. Just harvested today," Hannah said, spearing one from the pan with a fork. The mushroom was halfway in her mouth when Nate's hand shot out and knocked the fork clear out of her hand.

"What are you doing?" she cried out.

Nate pushed right past her, grabbed a sauté pan in each hand, and raced to the door. He kicked it open, then dumped the sizzling mushrooms over the porch railing.

13

Deep Freeze

"What are you doing? Are you insane?" Chef Cadot bellowed, charging onto the porch after Nate.

Nate flung both frying pans onto a wooden table over by the porch rail. He faced Cadot, his nose only inches from the chef's face. "Saving your stupid life," he hollered back. "Not that I should bother! Mr. Expert French Cook here knows everything there is to know about mushrooms. Right?"

Cadot backed away. Nancy could see he was intimidated.

"What are you trying to tell us?" Nancy asked.

He shifted his gaze to Nancy. "Well, little lady, it's all about the mushrooms. This idiot here was about to poison everyone."

"*Poison?*" Several voices gasped at once.

135

"These are not poisonous. You are a madman. Yes. You are mad!" Bristling, Cadot stomped back into the kitchen. He returned with the bowl of mushrooms Ryan had just cleaned, but hadn't yet sliced. He poked it under Nate's nose. "Show me!" He took a handful of the mushrooms and let them spill slowly from his palm. "Show me the poison."

Abruptly he cut himself off, still holding one mushroom. Like many of the others, it was tan, and it had a rough surface. "He eeez right. Zees will make people very ill. There are more of them here. Zee mushroom is called *Scleroderma citrinum.*"

"An earthball?!" Naomi cried, instantly recognizing the Latin name. "No way. Let me see. I culled *everything* I picked today. Ryan helped me. Right, Ryan?"

Ryan took the mushroom out of Cadot's hand. He looked at it, and his face registered pure horror. "I don't believe this. I don't know how I could miss this."

"We didn't miss just one of them," Naomi said in a quiet, shaky voice. Nancy quickly turned her attention from Ryan to Naomi. The girl wasn't just shocked, she was scared. "There are four or five in this bowl alone. How did they get here? I'm sure I didn't pick these."

"Someone did," Nancy commented. As Cadot began culling the poison ones, Nancy looked closely at the mushrooms. To her untrained eye, they all looked alike.

"Well, it had to be you, Naomi," Ryan said. "I only picked a few of the puffballs before I left to help prepare for lunch. But anyway, look—it's a very common mistake."

"Not one I would make, though," Naomi said, her cheeks beginning to redden.

At that moment Jillian intervened. "Obviously this wasn't intentional. Chef Cadot told us earlier that collecting wild mushrooms is tricky business. Naomi, no one blames you. Very glad we caught this though."

"We should serve something else tonight," Mike suggested to Cadot.

Lauren nodded. "We can't afford any more problems with our guests. And goodness knows this mistake could have cost someone their life—or at least their good health."

"*Our* guests!?" Jillian blurted. "Last I heard you were just helping in the kitchen until the chef's hand healed. You're supposed to be making a video, not running this place. Gourmet Getaway isn't your project anymore, Lauren."

"Well, *excuse* me!" Lauren countered snidely. "If it weren't for me, this video crew wouldn't be here to film the place and give you free publicity. Nor, I might add, would you have a food critic on the premises."

"A food critic?" Cadot gasped.

Mike looked concerned. "You're not supposed to know about that. None of us are."

Jillian ignored both men, but continued glowering

at Lauren. "Funny how your critic has turned up on what's proving to be the most disastrous week we've ever experienced. Maybe you planned to have this place be at its worst just when your pet critic is here? If the critic is indeed here."

"Enough!" Mike shouted, stepping between the two women. "Haven't we got enough problems without you two starting to go at each other again? Nate just saved us from some very serious trouble."

Nancy offered her hand to Nate. "I'm sure we're all grateful," she said. He didn't say anything, but his handshake was firm and direct.

At that moment Nancy realized that Mike was right. Nate had a beef with the Getaway, no doubt about it. But he wasn't the type to resort to sabotage. He'd start a fight face-to-face, bully you out of town if he had to—but he was an up-front, honest sort of guy. A character, but not a criminal. After all, he had just saved Hannah and a lot of Mike's customers from serious mushroom poisoning. He'd forestalled yet another Getaway disaster. Nancy dropped him from her list of suspects.

"Nate, I swear I'll put a stop to the problems with your traps. I disapprove of trapping, but you've got legal rights here. I'll see to it that no one bothers you again," Mike promised.

As Nate left, though, Mike cast a helpless glance at Nancy. "How I'm going to do *that*, I haven't the foggiest," he admitted to Nancy in an undertone. "I need to see you alone later this afternoon. Come to my office, off the kitchen. We can talk in private."

Cadot interrupted their conversation by herding everyone back into the kitchen. "We must rethink dinner quickly, *mes amis*. Perhaps we use more of those wonderful dried morels. . . ."

Later that afternoon Nancy passed through the main dining room on her way to Mike's kitchen office. She was curious about what he wanted to discuss. Had he stumbled on some new lead? Her own list of suspects was shrinking.

Given what had been going on at the Getaway, it was hard to imagine the poison mushrooms had turned up in the kitchen by accident. Just as unbelievable was that Naomi and Ryan had both overlooked them.

As she neared the passageway that linked the dining room with the kitchen she heard a woman's voice. "I won't be any part of this!"

Nancy recognized the voice. It belonged to Naomi. But to whom was she talking? Nancy tiptoed closer to the swinging door, hoping to hear more.

A man was saying something back to her. His tone was threatening, but he spoke too softly for Nancy to make out the words—or determine who was doing the talking.

"Let go of me!" Naomi's muffled cry was followed by the sound of something ripping. "You creep!" she cried. Suddenly she burst through the door, sobbing and tearing off her apron.

"Naomi?" Nancy called to her.

Naomi stopped short, clearly shocked to see Nancy. She looked back over her shoulder toward the passage. When she faced Nancy again, she looked like she wanted to say something. Before any words came out, thought, she shut her mouth.

Nancy's voice was gentle. "What's wrong? I'm going to see Mike. Do you want to come with me?"

Naomi looked petrified. "No. Please just tell him I quit. I can't work here anymore."

"Because of that fiasco with the mushrooms?" Nancy asked. "Anyone could make a mistake like that." *If it was a mistake,* Nancy added silently.

"The mushrooms?" The words hung on her lips. She rubbed her arm across her eyes, wiping away her tears. To her dismay, Nancy saw that the sleeve of Naomi's white blouse was torn. That explained that ripping sound. "You think *that's* why I'm quitting?" Naomi shot Nancy a look of total distaste. "You think I picked those mushrooms? You're dead wrong!"

Naomi was clearly insulted and hurt. Nancy waited for her to say more. After a second's silence, Naomi lifted her shoulders. "It's not the mushrooms. I had nothing to do with that. I just can't take working around all the meat. It's against my principles. Yes, that's it," she said. She sounded as if she were improvising. "Tell Mike that." She started off, then abruptly looked back. "Tell him nothing bad's going to happen here again."

"Naomi!" Nancy's heart sank as she watched her go. The girl clearly knew something about how those mushrooms got into the kitchen. She had hinted about it just now with her unusual behavior.

A noise in the passageway behind her suddenly caught her attention. Someone was still there. Nancy swiftly pushed open the swinging door. Ryan stood on the other side, holding a stack of dishes.

"How long have you been here?" She wondered what he'd overheard.

Ryan looked taken aback. "Well, hi to you too," he said. "I'm supposed to be helping Naomi set the tables for dinner."

"You're too late," Nancy told him. "She just quit."

"No way!" Ryan looked astounded. "Why'd she go and do a thing like that? You'd think she was afraid folks believe she picked those mushrooms on purpose."

"Do you think that?" Nancy was quick to ask.

"Absolutely not," he said. "That girl couldn't hurt a flea. But she's been spaced out lately. Sort of nervous. I don't know. She might have been careless this time, I guess. This wild game week is getting to her."

If Naomi had just been careless, though, Nancy thought, *then why didn't Ryan spot the bad mushrooms?*

"The events around here lately are probably getting to her," Nancy said. "Anyway, did you see someone come through here just now?"

Ryan shook his head. "Not a soul. But then, I just arrived." He turned to put the dishes on a shelf. Nancy stared at his back. Dangling out of the back pocket of his jeans was a piece of white cotton fabric—and it matched Naomi's shirt.

Nancy quickly realized that it was Ryan with whom Naomi had been fighting. And for some reason he was lying about it.

Had Naomi confronted him about the mushrooms? Had she threatened to expose him? Nancy suddenly recalled Bess's comment on their first night at the Getaway—something about Naomi being under Ryan's spell. Nancy suspected it had more to do with fear than romance. Nancy pondered this as she left Ryan and continued through the short passageway. In the kitchen, dinner preparation was in full swing. Nancy scooted past Cadot and moved into the hall that led to the pantry.

Just as she reached the office, Mike hurried in from the back porch. "Sorry I'm late." He tossed a clipboard on his desk. His tiny office had been carved out of what once was a storeroom. It was crammed with file cabinets, shelves full of cookbooks, and a computer table. His desk was piled with various ledgers.

"Now where's Jillian?" he asked, pulling the door shut behind him. It was heavy and closed with a loud bang. "I should wait for Jillian," Mike said as he cleared off a chair for Nancy. "I wanted her to be here. That incident with the mushrooms—I think it narrows the suspect list down some, don't you?"

"More than some," Nancy said, hearing a thumping against the wall. "What was that?" she asked, looking at the bookcase behind Mike's chair.

"I have no idea," Mike said as the sound started up again—only this time, it was louder. Nancy followed Mike over to the bookcase. She pressed her ear against the narrow strip of wall between the bookcase and the door. "Mike, what's on the other side of this wall?"

"The walk-in refrigerator . . . ," Mike responded in a grave voice.

"Someone must be trapped in there. I think I just heard a voice!"

14

Proof of the Pudding

"The latch must have slipped," Mike said as he and Nancy hurried out of the room. The office door slammed shut behind them. "It's supposed to have a safety device, but it's broken a couple of times already. We'd better get whoever it is out fast, before the person freezes."

The walk-in refrigerator was just to the right of the office. Tall metal storage shelves flanked either side of the thick refrigerator door. Made entirely of thick wood, the door was reinforced by rows of steel straps. Nancy read the sign posted to the door. WARNING: PROP DOOR OPEN WHEN INSIDE. LATCH IS—

Before Nancy could finish reading the sign, Mike grabbed her arm. "Now would you look at this!" He pointed to the handle of the door. The

144

latch was lowered, and the door was padlocked.

"Is there a key?" she asked Mike.

"Yes. The key ring's in my office. I do use this pad-lock sometimes," he admitted, "when we've had a big delivery, and if Jillian and I both have to be away for a good part of the day, or—" A faint cry of help cut off Mike's next words. "It sounds like Lauren!" He gasped.

Then he turned to the opposite wall. "Nancy— she's in there without a coat. Look!"

Nancy followed the direction of his gaze. Hanging from a row of hooks on the wall was Lauren's coat and cap. Next to it was Jillian's Norwegian ski sweater. "Were either Jillian or Lauren in the freezer this morning?" she asked as Mike hurried into his office.

"Sure. The food delivery came early, while you guys were out jogging. Since the chef is out of com-mission, they were both helping sort the order. When Monica raised the hue and cry, they were putting some stuff away in the kitchen, and storing the meat and fish out here."

Nancy filed that information away while Mike went to retrieve the keys. This probably meant she could rule out two more suspects. Neither woman could have been at the porch at the time of the assault.

A second later Mike burst out of the office. "I don't believe this. The key ring is missing."

"Which means whoever padlocked Lauren in

there probably still has the key." Nancy went over to the door. "Lauren?" she called, pounding on the heavy wood panels.

"Jillian?" Lauren's voice was louder now. "This has gone far enough."

"Jillian?" Mike and Nancy exclaimed in unison. At the sound of approaching footsteps, Nancy turned around. It was Jillian. She was partially hidden from Mike and Nancy by one of the metal shelves, but Nancy could see her clearly enough. The tall slim woman held a big brass key ring and wore a satisfied smirk on her face.

Jillian jangled the keys. "How ya doing Lauren?" she called out. "A good fifteen minutes in there should cool off your enthusiasm for trying to run this place. . . ." The words were scarcely out of her mouth when she spied Mike and Nancy. Her jaunty expression faded fast.

"You locked Lauren in there?" And for how long? Mike was incredulous. He grabbed the key ring from Jillian and began rummaging through the keys.

"Just long enough to teach her a lesson," Jillian said, the confidence leaking out of her voice. Nancy noticed her eyes were filling with water—and were already red from crying.

Mike finally located the key to the refrigerator and unlocked the door. Lauren came stumbling out, her face red from the cold, her whole body shaking.

"Thank—thank good—goodness that office door b-b-banged. I knew someone might f-f-finally hear me."

The moment Lauren set eyes on Jillian, her face flashed anger. Nancy was sure if Lauren hadn't been so cold and nearly frostbitten she would have hurled herself on Jillian. "I—I—can't b-b-believe you—you—did th-th-that!" Lauren declared through chattering teeth.

"Me neither, Jillian. What's going on here?!" Mike asked.

As Nancy grabbed Lauren's coat and threw it over the woman's shoulders, Mike steered her into the kitchen. On his way he looked back at Jillian. His expression was a mixture of horror and dismay. "Jillian, why in the world would you try to sabotage this place?"

Jillian let out a little cry and put her hand over her mouth. Lauren's jaw dropped. The two women looked at each other. "Me?" Jillian finally exclaimed. "You think *I* sabotaged the Gourmet Getaway?"

Lauren looked from Jillian to Mike, then back to Jillian again. Then she shook her head vehemently. "For Pete's sake, Mike. Get real here. We just had a fight—that's all. You saw the start of it this morning."

So, Nancy thought, *it was Jillian and Lauren I saw with Mike through the window.* The argument had been pretty heated. Nancy turned her attention back to Lauren, who was still talking to Mike.

"You think it's easy for me seeing you two make a go of it here. Jillian's right—I *would* like to be running

147

this place. This was *my* dream too—not just yours, Mike. Maybe I should have stayed away at least until I got over your starting the Getaway with a new wife! I said some mean things to Jillian this morning in the kitchen, and they clearly made her mad."

Jillian looked down at her shoes. "Mike, I'm sorry. I acted childishly." She shrugged. "Lauren, I'm sorry. I was way out of line. I wouldn't have let you get hurt or sick or anything though—you know that."

"Yeah, I know," Lauren said. Then she turned to Mike. "And *you* better know that neither of us are out to get you or are trying to make this business fail."

Nancy cleared her throat. "Lauren's right. If Jillian locked Lauren up about ten minutes ago or so, neither could be the culprit."

All eyes turned toward Nancy. "Do you know who's behind this?" Lauren sounded skeptical.

"I'm *almost* sure," Nancy said. "I just have to check something out before it gets dark."

Mike went to brew tea in the kitchen for the two women, and Nancy left to get George and Bess. She found them in the lounge playing a computer game. It took only a second to convince them to abandon their game and help her with her investigation.

"I just wish you'd tell us whom you suspect," Bess prodded as she buttoned up her jacket.

"Not yet. Your job—and George's—is to search the inn and the grounds for a pair of discarded boots."

"Rubber boots?" George asked as the three girls walked down the back hall to the porch.

"No, work or hiking boots."

"Like the boots Ryan wears," Bess said slowly. "You don't think . . ."

"Lots of people wear the kind of boots he wears," George pointed out. "Naomi has some, and so do half the members of the video crew. *Monica* even has a pair—she was waterproofing them the other day on the back porch."

"We can rule out the video crowd," Nancy said, pulling on her gloves. "They turned up *after* the first incident, the power outage. We're looking for boots, or bootlike shoes, with red paint stains. Whoever tacked those pheasant feathers to the chef's door also stepped in the paint. I'm sure the soles of the boots will be stained."

Nancy divided up the territory to be searched. George would scope out the chicken house, barn, and riding stable. Nancy would concentrate on the yard around the chef's cottage, the compost area, and the garbage bins. Bess opted to search the storage rooms and the pantry. They agreed to meet back at the kitchen porch in an hour, just before dark.

Clouds were lowering as Nancy poked around the mulch in the chef's garden. She turned up nothing. From the garden she went over to the composting area. Naomi had shown it to the group during the wild-food tour. She'd also shown them various tool sheds where garden equipment was kept, but she'd avoided one building. It was small, and painted green. It almost looked like a converted outhouse. When Nancy approached it, she saw the door was secured with only a small latch.

The shed was dark inside. In the dim light coming through the door, she saw a pile of burlap sacks, nothing more. She was about to leave when she saw something metal glinting beneath one of the bags. Gingerly she pulled back the sack, revealing a jumble of wood and metal. Nancy recognized it instantly: one of Nate's traps. And it was dismantled. Nancy pulled off the rest of the sacks. Sure enough, there were about a half dozen broken traps.

The sight saddened Nancy. She had hoped that Naomi was innocent—but it looked like this wasn't the case.

After carefully checking the shed for the boots, Nancy closed the door. She'd tell Mike about her findings as soon as she got back to the inn. Quickly she investigated the garbage bins. They'd been emptied that morning, so there was little inside. When she walked around the back of the farthest bin, however, she practically tripped on a soggy brown paper sack—and her toe hit something hard.

She bent down and looked inside. "Yes!" she cried aloud. She'd found the workboots. They were smelly, and the toe ends of both boots were badly worn. Nancy turned them over. The soles were covered with grass, debris—and streaks of red paint. The boots were too large for a woman. They had to be a men's size 11 or 12. It was Nancy's guess they'd be the perfect size for Ryan.

Feeling vindicated, Nancy rewrapped the boots in the soggy brown paper and tucked the bundle under her arm. She headed back toward the kitchen convinced that she'd tracked down the vandal—hopefully in time to prevent another incident.

As she approached the inn Nancy thought she saw someone slip behind the side of the back porch. Curious, Nancy decided to see who it was. At the root cellar she could hear someone pounding on the door. The entrance to the cellar lay practically even with the ground. It resembled the doors to storm cellars in houses in the Midwest, where tornadoes are a threat. As Nancy looked, the door shook again. There was no mistaking it—someone was inside.

Nancy bent down to pull it open. She saw that the latch was shut. Then she heard Bess's voice. "Get me out of here. Help! Someone."

"Bess!" Nancy cried out. She yanked open the latch and pulled the door handle. The door flew open to reveal Bess standing on the bottom concrete step. Tears were flooding her face.

"Nancy," Bess cried in a panicky voice. "It's Ryan!"

She coughed and choked on her tears. Nancy started down the steps to help her friend up. "I ran into him in the pantry and told him we were looking for the boots. He suggested I try down here, and then . . ." Bess broke down again. "He locked me in here, Nancy. Then I dropped my flashlight, and . . ." Bess broke off, and her blue eyes grew huge with fright.

"*Nan, watch out!*" she shouted—but a moment too late. Nancy felt a fist punch her from behind. Nancy went flying down the steps, knocking Bess right over. The dirt floor and some sacks cushioned their fall.

Nancy lay stunned for a second. She jumped up and spun around just in time to see a flash of blond hair. Then the cellar door slammed, and they heard the latch drop. She and Bess were trapped.

15

... Into the Fire

"Bess, are you all right?" Nancy asked. She felt along the floor. Her fingers first encountered stacks of burlap sacks, like the ones they had landed on. Then she touched Bess's hand.

"Y-Yesss," Bess replied, sounding unsure of herself. She gripped Nancy's hand, and added, "Good thing the floor's not too hard here."

"It's dirt, and this stack of potato sacks is practically as thick as a mattress," Nancy told her, fishing for her penlight in her pocket. Once she had it in her hand, she flicked it on. Bess was sitting up, rubbing her arms, looking desolate but okay. Nancy scrambled to her feet and examined their surroundings. "Let's try to find the light switch," she told Bess.

Nancy quickly found Bess's flashlight. When she

tried to turn it on, thought, it wouldn't work. Nancy shook it. Something rattled inside the lamp. "The bulb must have broken when you dropped it, Bess."

Nancy moved to the center of the room and aimed the penlight at the ceiling.

By now Bess was on her feet. "Nan—what's this string do?" she asked. Nancy looked up above her head to where Bess was pointing.

"Good for you. That's the pull cord for the light bulb." The string was short—too short for Bess to reach. Standing on tiptoe, Nancy was able to grab it. She pulled, but nothing happened.

"That bulb's blown too! Just our luck," Bess said.

Nancy aimed her light higher. The light's beam was narrow, but she could see that there was no bulb in the socket in the ceiling.

A shiver ran down Nancy's spine. Ryan was more devious and far smarter than Nancy had given him credit for. He wasn't just some animal rights activist acting on emotional impulse. The guy planned his sabotage like a professional criminal. "I bet he was just waiting for Jillian's next tour of the cellar to lock the guests in the dark—to create another scene and scare them to death."

"Well," Bess said woefully, "it's working. I'm scared."

"Well, I'm mad!" Nancy declared. She marched past Bess and up to the cellar door. She began to pound on it. "Someone's got to hear us," she told Bess.

"Why?" Bess asked. "You probably never toured this cellar. I did, the first day I went to a cooking class. Monsieur Cadot wanted to show us the proper way to store roots. It turns out the only opening to this room is that cellar door. The old entrances are behind walls now. No one upstairs can hear us. And who's hanging out in the barnyard now, aside from Ryan."

Bess had a point. And Ryan probably knew there was only one way out. Nancy's heart sank. But wait—hadn't Jillian mentioned another entrance during the kitchen tour? With any luck, Ryan might not have known it even existed, so he wouldn't have thought to block it. Nancy started back down the steep short flight of concrete steps.

An acrid odor wafted toward her. "Ugh, what's that smell?" she asked.

Bess sniffed. "Nan"—Bess paused and sniffed again—"we've got a bigger problem than being locked in. That's smoke. There's a fire somewhere!"

Nancy's heart began to race. A fire—and no escape route.

"Nancy, what are we going to do?"

Bess's wail catapulted Nancy into action. "We are going to get out of here. Ryan Logan isn't going to get the better of us, Bess." After a moment she realized the smoke was coming from just outside. The cellar door was wooden, but it was thick and damp

155

from the other night's storm. It wouldn't burn fast. She had a little time to find a way out. That is, if the smoke didn't get much worse.

Nancy thought quickly. Taking off her sweatshirt, she tied one sleeve around her wrist and handed the other sleeve to Bess. "Hold on tight, and don't let go," she ordered. "The smoke's going to get worse before we get out of here. We might lose each other. Let's stay close to the ground and try to find another way out. I'm sure there's some way back up toward the pantry and the kitchen. In the old days people wouldn't have wanted to go outside to get to the root cellar in winter." With feigned confidence, Nancy kept assuring Bess. "We'll find some way up."

Nancy looked around quickly. She spotted some old tools over by the steps. Most of them looked rusty, but there were a couple of screwdrivers that still looked useful. She picked the tools up and tucked them in the back pockets of her jeans.

Nancy carefully made her way toward the back of the cellar. With each passing second the smoke grew thicker. Behind her, Bess was coughing. Nancy stopped a moment, licked her finger, and held it up. She hoped to feel a draft. Luckily there was the weakest current of air coming from somewhere to her right.

Nancy started toward what she hoped was the source of the faint breeze. Suddenly her penlight died.

Bess tugged on her end of Nancy's sweatshirt. "Nancy! The smoke's worse, and now we can't see a thing."

"Let's just keep on going," Nancy told her. She put out her hand and groped in the dark. Before the penlight died, she had seen something that might be a hole in the wall. "Bess, hang in there a minute longer. I think I found a way out of here." Half shuffling, half stumbling, she finally encountered a cold brick wall. The smoke had gathered here and was heavier. With every breath Nancy's lungs began to burn. Nancy crouched down, trying to get below the curtain of smoke. With her free hand she felt along the base of the wall.

At first the bricks seemed to continue without a break. Then suddenly Nancy's fingers encountered empty space. Carefully she reached forward. Her hand touched something wooden and vertical—the riser on a step. Nancy almost cheered. "Bess, I found stairs." Nancy explored the step with her hand. There was another step above it. Relief washed over her. "And they go up. Come on."

"I can't. I'm afraid." Bess sounded hysterical. She was coughing and crying. "The smoke's worse here!"

Nancy turned around and tugged on the sweatshirt. She could barely make out Bess's form through the thickening haze. Nancy reached back, grabbed Bess's arm, and forcibly began to pull her onto the steps. "Trust me," she told Bess. Slowly she managed to guide Bess through the dark smoke and up the stairs. As they reached the top they could hear the sound of sirens.

Nancy felt a surge of hope.

"There's a door!" Bess exclaimed, reaching the top a second before Nancy. She sounded extremely happy. Nancy heard Bess pound on the door. "But it won't open."

"It's probably locked." But with any luck it would have the same sort of metal latch as all the other old doors around the farm. By now she knew how to deal with those. She'd need a tool. She remembered the screwdrivers in her pockets. One of them had seemed pretty sturdy. Nancy took the screwdriver and worked it under the latch. The latch was so brittle that as Nancy tried to pry it open, it broke right off. She threw herself against the door, and it moved slightly.

"Bess," she cried, "with our combined body weight against it, I think the door will open."

Bess and Nancy squeezed together on the narrow top step. "On the count of three . . . ," Nancy ordered. "One . . . two . . . three." At once they both flung themselves at the door. The girls stumbled into a twist of charred and broken shelves and a thick curtain of smoke. Nancy gasped for air. "We're in the pantry!" she cried.

"Hey—there are a couple of girls here!" a husky male voice shouted. Strong hands grabbed Nancy. Another pair of arms went around Bess.

"Nancy—they're firemen!" Bess sounded positively blissful.

As Nancy stumbled out of the pantry and into the smoky kitchen, she managed to get some words out. "This fire is probably arson. And I'm pretty sure I know who set it." After a brief coughing fit, Nancy managed to get more words out. "It's Ryan. Ryan Logan."

"You sure?" Mike's voice broke through the smoke. He was right behind the firemen. The group of them helped Nancy and Bess out to the backyard.

Once outside, Nancy drew in some fresh air. Her eyes were streaming from the smoke, but within minutes she felt like she could breathe again. Two firetrucks were in the yard with their engines running and lights flashing. Their headlights made the evening nearly as bright as day.

"Nancy, you're sure it's Ryan?" Mike asked.

Nancy nodded. "I found his boots. They were stashed behind the Dumpster, stained with red paint. And this is just a bit of the evidence."

Mike looked relieved. "Do you think he was working alone?"

Nancy nodded. "I'm sure of it now. At first when I narrowed down the list of suspects, I thought Naomi was involved—"

Mike broke in. "But she wasn't?"

Before he could say another word, George ran up

to Nancy. "Nan, what happened? Are you okay?"

Nancy nodded. "A little smoky, but fine." She looked around. "Where is everybody?"

"Jillian and Lauren evacuated the building. They have the guests in the front of the property. The firemen will let them back in soon. Hannah's with them."

Nancy was relieved. At least Hannah and George were okay. And so was Mike. She saw him talking to the fireman—he looked furious. Nancy felt sorry for him. She hoped smoke damage from the fire was minimal.

She looked around for Naomi and Ryan, but they weren't around.

"What were you doing in the root cellar?" George asked as Bess walked up. Her face was a little sooty, but otherwise she looked okay.

"Ryan locked me in there. Nancy tried to rescue me, and he tricked her, too. Then the fire started," Bess told her.

"Unfortunately Ryan's boots are down there." Nancy looked over at the root cellar. "They were covered with paint. I feel so ridiculous; I actually saw him carrying them in a brown sack over toward the garbage bins. But I didn't connect that with the missing boots. At least not until we saw his new ones at the town meeting."

"You knew it was Ryan even then?" Bess was amazed. "Why didn't you warn me?"

Nancy threw her arm around Bess and gave her a

hug. "First, you wouldn't have believed me. Second, I wasn't sure yet if he was working alone."

George nodded. "He wasn't my top suspect. Nate was. As for Ryan's boots, don't worry, Nan—the evidence will still be down in the root cellar. The fire's out. Pretty soon the firemen will go down there. There were two fires, really," George told Nancy. "One outside the root cellar door, and one in the pantry."

Nancy shuddered. If either blaze had gotten out of control, she and Bess would have been in serious trouble. No one would have thought to look for them in the root cellar.

Mike walked up to Nancy. "Thank goodness you're okay, Nancy. That was a close call," he said. "The good news is that no one's hurt, and there hasn't been much damage. Even the kitchen is fairly unscathed. The pantry fire was set in a garbage can. We were able to drag it outside pretty fast. Some shelves broke and there's a lot of smoke damage, but it's mainly only in that room. As for the root cellar, we'll air it out. We didn't have much stored in it yet this year."

At the sound of approaching sirens, Nancy's ears perked. Two patrol cars pulled into the yard. Troopers climbed out, and one of them disappeared into the chef's cottage. A moment later he emerged holding Ryan by the scruff of the neck. Ryan's hands were handcuffed behind his back. His eyes met Nancy's, his expression still defiant.

The state trooper announced, "Here's your man. And your woman." He gestured with his head to a slender figure standing on the top of Chef Cadot's steps. It was Naomi. Nancy didn't know if she was arrested yet or not. "She turned him in—told us the whole story," the trooper said.

Naomi took a deep breath, squared her shoulders, and came down the steps. She headed toward Mike and the others. Nancy motioned for George and Bess to follow her. She joined the little group just as Naomi was beginning to tell her story.

"Mike, you're not going to believe me. And I don't blame you if you don't. But I really had no idea Ryan would go this far."

"How are you connected with Ryan?" the trooper asked Naomi.

Naomi shrugged. "He turned up at our Save the Wildlife meetings a few months ago. He seemed to be experienced at peaceful protest. He knew more than most people around here about how to get our point across without going outside the boundaries of the law. In the past he'd traveled where there was a problem and tried to stir things up peacefully. What we didn't know is that he's also part of an extremist animal rights and environmental group—the kind that believes in arson and sabotage and even murder to prove their point." Naomi's voice quavered.

Nancy took pity on her. "But *you* don't believe in that?"

Naomi's head snapped up. "No, I don't. Not at all. You know I don't," she said to Nancy.

"But why didn't you come to me, Naomi," Mike said sternly. "You obviously suspected he was behind all our troubles here."

"Not at first. I really didn't." Naomi lowered her eyes and blushed. "Ryan's such a sweet-talking guy. I looked up to him . . . believed in him. Anyway, I thought the power outage was an accident. And when Cadot was in town—that stoning business didn't seem so bad to me. What happened in the store—it must have been Ryan who knocked the shelf over— *that* was scary. I thought Ryan was beginning to lose it." Naomi ran her hand through her hair and looked very distraught. "I think part of me had already figured out it was Ryan. But it wasn't until that awful mess he made with the paint and pheasant feathers that I knew things had gone too far."

"You mentioned that—I remember. I thought maybe you were just feeling sick at the sight of the feathers," Nancy said.

Naomi shook her head. "But that glove business *did* freak me out. I found the other glove in the locker room later, stuffed behind Ryan's locker. I confronted him, and he threatened me. He told me if I exposed him, well . . . I don't know. He made it sound scary."

The trooper looked at Naomi. "What made you come to us, then?"

Naomi's answer was instant. "The mushrooms! That was awful. He obviously had picked a bunch of poisonous earthballs on his way back here from our harvesting expedition today. He somehow kept them separate from the rest of the mushrooms until Hannah was actually cooking. People could have gotten *really* sick if Nate hadn't walked in when he did. What in the world was Ryan thinking?" Naomi burst into tears.

"That zee end justifies zee means."

Nancy turned around. Chef Cadot was standing there with his arms folded across his chest, studying Naomi. "That took courage, Mademoiselle Naomi—to go to the police." He turned to Mike. "Perhaps you may want to fire her after zees, but I think she would be good to have here. She does understand zee wild harvest—and I trust her, Rinaldi."

"So you aren't going to press charges against me?" Naomi looked flabbergasted.

Mike shook his head. "Ryan's the bad guy here. You might sympathize with some of his views, but that's not a crime."

Naomi caught Nancy's eye and swallowed hard. Nancy could see from her expression that she realized Nancy knew about the traps.

"About the shed, Naomi . . . ," Nancy prompted.

Naomi nodded. "Nancy's right. There's more to it. Ryan didn't sabotage Nate's traps. I did. They're all in that shed behind the chef's cottage. Nancy'll show you where." Naomi hesitated. "So I guess you'll press charges now? Or at least fire me."

Mike thought a minute. "No. I won't do either. Chef Cadot thinks you're an asset to this place, and I'd agree. The business with the traps—that's serious. You will have to make restitution to Nate—pay him enough to buy or make new traps."

Naomi cringed at the thought. After a second, though, she nodded her head. "Okay," she said in a soft voice. "I'll do that."

"Good. So you still work here, and now I will put you to zee work," Cadot declared. "I need your help because this hand is still useless. We will make tonight pizza—vegetarian ones with Naomi's help. We will also make one with my special venison sausage. We will make dinner—how do you say?— buffet style. Everyone here is invited."

The firemen and state troopers thanked Cadot, but explained that they were on duty. Mike arranged for the pizzas to be delivered to the firehouse and police station later.

While the chef went back into the kitchen, Nancy spoke to the troopers. She told them where to find the ax and Ryan's boots.

As she had obviously been the target of some of Ryan's attacks, they asked her to come to the station in the morning and fill out a report. In the meantime, they told her, she should relax and enjoy dinner.

The impromptu buffet supper was a huge hit. Savory pizzas and other dishes were piled on long tables in the dining room. A buffet of sweets and desserts was displayed in the lounge. Getaway guests seemed to be enjoying the more casual atmosphere. Meanwhile Lauren's crew was in major interview mode. They were filming almost everyone in sight—including Monica.

Nancy hung out with Bess and George in a corner of the lounge far from the cameras, observing the scene from a distance. As they ate they watched Jillian, then Mike, and then various guests parade in front of the cameras. The guests all told their stories of how a quiet weekend at the Gourmet Getaway had turned into their most memorable vacation. Cadot kept coming in from the kitchen with new dishes. He led the cameraman over to film each one before the diners disturbed his lovely presentations.

Nancy was happy, but exhausted. A shower and a nap before dinner had partially revived her, but she was more in the mood for popcorn and a video than a big public dinner.

Bess nudged Nancy. "Surprise, surprise!" Bess said, gesturing toward Monica. "She was ready to hightail it out of here from the minute she arrived. Seems she's changed her mind. That woman really loves the camera."

"She actually seems to be thriving on the publicity," George quipped, devouring her third piece of Monsieur Cadot's secret recipe roast chicken.

"That's because the woman is ready for prime time," Bess observed. "Look at her. That hair is really too good to be true. When she learned she could be one of the stars of this video, she put her best foot forward."

"I'm surprised she's doing an interview," Nancy remarked. "She seemed, well . . . a sort of private person," Nancy said, just to see her friends' reaction.

"More like a snob," George contradicted. "But the way she carried on in the dining room when they found that glove in the pheasant—she seemed like an aspiring soap opera actress. This could be her big moment!"

Nancy felt sorry for Monica—or rather, Sylvia, whom she suspected was a very nice person trapped in the role of the snob this weekend. Still, George had a point. Nancy was still smiling over George's remark when Monica casually sauntered up. "Nice spread," she said. "Nancy, come with me to the buffet table and tell me what's *really* edible."

Nancy followed the woman. En route to the dining room, Monica steered Nancy into the back hall.

"I just wanted to thank you," she said warmly, "for keeping my secret."

"What secret?" Nancy winked. "Though I must say, I know Bess and Hannah would die to find out who you really are. Speaking of which, how's the review going—or shouldn't I ask? And does anyone ever really know your true identity when you review restaurants?"

Monica rolled her eyes. "I haven't finished the review yet—and my deadline's in three days. I'll have to e-mail it to my editor. We've decided to stay on here until next weekend. It'll be a good review. In spite of all the disruptions, the food was great, the management was flexible and accommodating, and Mike is, well, a very good and patient host." She hesitated. "And as for the 'real identity,' I'm afraid my cover will be blown for good when *Offbeat* comes out. It's a quarterly, and the next issue closes this week to be published next month. My picture will grace the front page of the article." Nancy couldn't wait to see her friends' reactions.

"Oh," Monica said as Hannah, Bess, and George approached. "Here come your friends."

"Nancy!" Hannah said in an excited whisper. "I figured it all out."

"What?"

"Who the critic is!" Bess blurted, then she saw Monica. "Oh well, I guess I let the cat out of the bag. But who cares now. Monica, you will not believe this.

There's a food critic here, and he's been here all weekend—through every single one of the Getaway's disasters!"

"Really?" Monica caught Nancy's eye.

"Yes," Hannah proclaimed. "And it's him." She pointed to Oscar Sanchez. He was strolling out of the dining room toward the lounge with a generous plateful of food.

"Oscar?" Monica was stunned.

"Why him?" Nancy asked.

"Nancy, I'm surprised at you. Didn't you notice how he was sampling everyone's dish at his table at *every* meal? Critics do that, you know. They always have dinner partners, and they like to taste just about everything on the menu. This tendency of his was a dead giveaway. Besides, he's also a bit portly—which makes me think he does this often."

Monica's eyes grew wide. As Nancy met her glance, they both broke into laughter.

"What's so funny?" George wondered out loud.

"Let's look at next month's *Offbeat and Great Eats* magazine," Nancy suggested, "to see if Detective Hannah's theory is right—and find out if we broke our record for the number of cases cracked on a vacation!"